DATE NIGHT

6

DATE NIGHT

CARMEN GREEN

sepia

BET BOOKS™

BET Publications, LLC
www.bet.com

SEPIA BOOKS are published by

BET Publications, LLC
c/o BET BOOKS
One BET Plaza
1900 W Place NE
Washington, DC 20018-1211

All Kensington Titles, Imprints, and Distributed Lines are available at special quantity discounts for bulk purchases for sales promotions, premiums, fund-raising, and educational or institutional use. Special book excerpts or customized printings can also be created to fit specific needs. For details, write or phone the office of the Kensington special sales manager: Kensington Publishing Corp., 850 Third Avenue, New York, NY 10022, attn: Special Sales Department, Phone: 1-800-221-2647.

ISBN: 1-58314-294-0

First Printing: September 2004
10 9 8 7 6 5 4 3 2 1

Printed in the United States of America

To Lisa Avery;
this one's for you.

Chapter 1
BJ

"What did those heffas say when you told them you weren't even close to getting married?"

BJ looked over at her best friend of two years, Marquita Snell, and didn't answer. The "heffas" she derisively referred to had been BJ's fellow WNBA teammates and best girlfriends until she'd retired two years ago. Then she'd all but disappeared from their lives. *And they from hers.* "I told them I'd just broken up with someone."

BJ stood on her custom-built basketball court outside of her half-million-dollar home and tossed in balls while Quita sat on the retractable bleachers. Although BJ had had the good sense to remove her red heels as soon as she'd gotten in from the wedding of former Flames point guard Terri Busche-Smith, the red-and-black silk dress that swirled around her legs hadn't been so lucky.

When she'd first arrived at the church, she'd been thrilled to see everyone, but that excitement quickly waned as they pressed her on the details of her personal life.

BJ tossed in four shots.

"You make more when you're mad."

"Shut up," BJ told Quita, and banged down another six. In defiance, she stopped shooting and dribbled for a minute. If what Quita

1

said was true, BJ had to ask herself if she was angry because all of her old friends had made a good transition into regular life, or because they viewed her life through rose-colored matrimonial glasses and found hers lacking.

"God, they make me sick." She tossed the ball into the air, jumped, and patted it in. "Where's Ebony? I thought she was coming with you."

"She had to take her evil mama to the doctor."

BJ looked at her watch. "This late?"

"The woman swore she was having a heart attack."

"Probably her guilty conscience. I'll call her tomorrow. I should have said I was engaged."

"What's the point of lying?" Quita sounded indignant. "I don't know why you didn't just tell them to mind their own damned business."

"First, I don't consider what I did lying; I was just avoiding a discussion I didn't want to have. And second, they're my friends. Getting defensive would have thrown up a red flag that says I'm not satisfied with my life."

"Are you?"

"Yeah." BJ tossed the ball toward the hoop and it smacked the backboard hard.

"Yeah, you reek of satisfaction," Quita retorted.

"I am!"

"Then what are you yelling for? Shit! I wish you could see yourself stomping around outside in your bare feet. It's not even sixty degrees out here, and you've destroyed a perfectly good silk dress. If you're so happy, then I'm Bozo the damn Clown."

BJ held the ball against her hip and breathed in deeply. She looked at Quita from the corner of her eye, then away. "I'm okay with myself, all right?"

"Different from happy, but an improvement." Quita wrapped an Atlanta Falcons blanket around her legs. "I'm wondering, why are they grillin' you about your love life? Every female in the world doesn't want to get married. Did that ever occur to them?"

"Of course not."

Because that's exactly what BJ wanted, too.

Nostalgia for the game, the girls, and the simplicity of her past had hit her hard this evening, and BJ couldn't understand why. She didn't miss the grueling schedule, or being poor as she had been until she'd made the pros.

Being a professional athlete had been a dream come true, but ever since she'd left the game, she'd been in a quandary over the next logical step in her life.

Her degree in early childhood education had been her backup to basketball, but she couldn't imagine her six-foot-one self in an elementary school chair. Her existence had always centered around the sport, and it was only fitting that she worked for the Atlanta Hawks as VP of public and community relations.

Tonight she'd seen firsthand that the women with whom she'd shared parallel lives for sixteen years had all changed. They were married, had children and nannies, and they sat on the boards of nonprofit organizations.

They weren't athletes anymore. She was the only one still hung up on an identity the others didn't seem to regret leaving behind.

Envy she'd never known rushed from its hiding place. She wanted their lives. But there wasn't a man on her horizon.

BJ let the basketball sail through the air, and it flicked the end of the net.

The game was still her first love.

"If talking to them bothers you so much, you should tell them to go to hell."

"Quita," BJ complained. "I'm not as cold about life as you." But tonight she'd wanted to be. The hopelessly ruined silk gripped her like wet tissue. "To be honest, in a small way, I want to be them." She adjusted the dress and bounced the ball between her legs.

"I never knew that." Quita got off the bleachers, her gray cargo capri pants and pink *Fame* skintight T-shirt more elegant looking than BJ's dress.

She teetered on Farragamo sandals, in defiance to the May wind. "That's because I never told anyone."

Quita gathered balls, the Falcons blanket now draped around her shoulders like a shawl. "Why?"

BJ didn't want to be so revealing, but tonight Quita was the only person in the world who wanted to listen. "I'm tall and I played professional basketball. People don't expect me to have the same dreams as they do. I still get the 'How's the air up there' jokes."

"I'd say 'the same as when you're unconscious. Wanna see first-hand?' People can be so stupid."

"You're my hero." BJ chuckled and stretched. The wind had picked up and chilled her skin.

She started to pull the ball rack off the court when a ball hit her in the back. "Hey!" She turned around. "What's your problem?"

"Don't be a smartass when I say I understand how you feel. We all have dreams, BJ. One day you might not agree with mine, but I damn sure want your respect."

BJ held her rare temper in check. "My mistake, but you couldn't just say that? That hurt."

Quita didn't blink as she walked into the house, leaving BJ outside. "So does letting your so-called friends ruin a day you've been looking forward to for months."

In that regard, she couldn't have been more right. BJ stood center court, alone. All the preparation for the wedding, getting her hair done, manicure and pedicure, and picking out the right dress and shoes had turned into a day she'd rather have skipped. But the day had culminated into one defining question. Would she find a man to love?

"Yes."

BJ looked up sharply. "What?"

"When you're worried, you mutter. Yes, we'll find two crazy but rich men to love us." Quita grinned from the door. "We'll even find one for Ms. Difficult, too."

"How can you be so sure? Especially about Ebony?" BJ smiled.

Quita's Philly-toughened voice softened. "Because God loves us."

"What? You believe in God now?"

"I've always believed in God—just not in church. Anyhow, He isn't mean just for the heck of it." She closed the sliding door.

The lingering question in her mind was had she exhausted her opportunities with God when she'd made the WNBA? She looked at her friend, who'd made herself comfortable in the kitchen.

What were Quita's dreams?

The glass door slid open. "Come on, the Jell-O shooters are ready."

"How's that solving our problem?"

Quita shrugged. "On a day like this, I think better when I'm a little drunk."

"We only get tipsy when we have something to celebrate."

Quita lifted a silver shooter cup. "Then drink up. I'm going to give you and Ebony a surprise."

BJ went inside and tossed back her spiked Jell-O. "What is it?"

"Don't rush me. Let's meet at Taboo next Friday, and I'll unveil our get-a-man plan."

Quita walked into the den and BJ stood in the kitchen.

A get-a-man plan? Why not? She had nothing to lose.

Chapter 2
BJ

Six-thirty didn't arrive quickly enough for BJ, as she sat on pins and needles at Taboo Bistro. She ordered her standard raspberry martini and appetizers, then settled back, letting the strains of jazz violinist Ed Forte soothe her stressed heart.

All day her thoughts had revolved around Quita's parting words from a week ago.

She hoped Quita would arrive first, but Ebony walked in wearing her standard evil expression, dressed in a severe gray suit and white blouse. Short, dark-skinned, and blunt, Ebony would have made a great dictator. But she'd been born in the twentieth century and the world had allowed men to become the ruling force. They were missing some raw talent.

Ebony looked at a man who was walking toward her. Midway, he made a U-turn and sat back down.

"Cruella, what you drinking?" BJ asked.

"Damn, what did he want? I just got here."

"Maybe sex, your number, your order, advice on what not to do to a woman, who the hell knows? How you doing?"

"Fine." Ebony got situated in a seat between the stage and a speaker. "You?"

"Glad it's Friday."

"Your day that bad?"

"The usual." BJ drained the remainder of her drink and signaled for another.

"Me, too. Stan can't get anything done without me, so I've been going in at seven-thirty every morning just to get the day off to a good start. Only, the more organized I am, the more work he needs done. I'm exhausted."

"Tell him you need an assistant."

Ebony shook her head and rubbed her carpal-tunnel-syndrome afflicted wrists. "He just laid off two people last month."

"Well, at least tell him he needs to take on more of the load instead of heaping it all on you. Tell him you'll quit otherwise."

"Right, and then I'll really be stuck with Mama and Aunt Jo forever. How was the wedding?"

"Good. Everybody was there. How's your mother?"

"Please, don't mention her while I'm trying to relax."

"Ebony," BJ chided.

"She ain't dead, okay? False alarm, as usual. We spent all night at the hospital to find out she has acid reflux. No surprise there, since she eats everything in sight."

"That can be painful."

Ebony's look could peel paint. BJ changed the subject. "I'm glad we decided to meet. We can have a mini investment-club meeting right here. Our investments are doing well."

"Quita left me a message that our new stock went up. She said it hit thirty-seven before slipping."

BJ nodded. "We still made a tidy sum. Here she comes now."

When Marquita Snell entered a room, men gawked. Tall and toasty brown, Quita was a showstopper. She wore beauty like a runway model. Her strides were long, and she gave men no play.

Those bold enough to approach were granted half a second, and if she wasn't interested, they became dust in the tail of her blazing comet. Quita didn't apologize for being direct or beautiful, and men worshipped her. "What are you staring at me like that for?" Marquita landed gracefully in her seat as she fingered over a waiter. "Hennessy and apple juice."

She crossed her legs and the waiter salivated until the bartender rang the bell, startling him. He stumbled away.

"Don't you see all these men with their tongues on the floor?" BJ ate a nacho, and savored the corn and salt.

If she chose to, she could feel like an ugly baby around Quita, but she didn't let the tinge of envy color her perspective. Men around the room lifted their glasses to her. They didn't even have the decency to cast a sympathy glance to BJ or Ebony.

"Whose tongues are on the floor?" Sex appeal oozed from her challenging tone. It had been that way since the three had met two years ago at an investment seminar at DeKalb College. Only now, since January first of this year, had their club been making money.

Ebony snapped her fingers in front of Quita. "Will you turn off the UPN-Quita network and tune in to the other people at this table?" Ebony tried to play it off, but the attention bothered her. "You don't have to be so obvious."

Quita didn't turn around to her newly delivered drink until she'd thoroughly examined every man in the room. "I thought the idea was to *get* them to look at us. Otherwise, we may as well be gay."

Ebony sucked her teeth. *"Not* me."

"Shut up, Quita," BJ said, before Ebony could launch into what promised to be a buzz-killing monologue.

She looked at Ebony. "You know she's just trying to get a rise out of you. Why do you always take the bait?"

"Because she's always making ridiculous statements. One day, somebody is going to take her seriously."

Quita sipped her drink. "When I get serious, I'll let you know."

Ed Forte took the stage for his second set and the music flowed over BJ. She needed this break. She wanted this Friday night to last at least three days, and the rest of the weekend to slip by as it may.

The acoustic guitar player winked at her and BJ kept the drink at her lips, replaying what just happened.

He took his fingers off the strings, pointed at her, and winked again.

A full-body flush started at her tingling scalp.

He was tall, bald, and had a handsome smile. A definite *maybe*. He went back to work and she diverted her attention, wondering *why me?*

She sipped her raspberry martini and let the spicy vodka light up her tongue as it slid warm and smooth down her throat.

She finally smiled at the percussionist and he grinned back.

A fine chocolate brotha with naturally curly hair and smooth skin waded into view, then passed a throng before claiming the only open seat at a table of eight.

Suddenly, every woman within a ten-foot radius transformed. Pelvic muscles contracted, nipples flipped on high beam, hair bounced, smiles appeared, and eyes flirted. The X chromosome was in full effect, and vied for the twenty-four-karat band of gold.

One man.

Thirty-three women.

And Quita.

BJ didn't consider herself or Ebony part of the mix.

Women simpered and leaned in, trying like hell to get his attention, but he had eyes for only one woman. Yet, that didn't stop a sista with regal fingers from tapping his shoulder.

"Excuse me, but what's your name? I'm Amethyst."

She'd made the first move. She'd staked her claim, and according to the rules of the street, the one who spoke first had first dibs—until he said otherwise. Not that Quita was giving him the attention. Her eyes were on the one unavailable man in the house. The handsome violinist.

"Jimmy," he answered, but leaned toward Quita. "I'm trying to get to know this young lady right here."

Quita cut her eyes at him and looked back at the stage.

BJ smirked at their stupidity as shoulders yanked back, hair stilled, and everyone's attention diverted back to the working brotha on stage.

The appetizers arrived, and Ebony and BJ ate while Jimmy tried to get to know Quita.

Ebony took out her calculator. "If our club keeps making money like we did this week, we should be able to retire by the time we're fifty."

Ebony had two philosophies on money: make it and save it, whereas BJ liked to live in relative comfort.

"Not quite where my thoughts were going today," BJ told her over the music.

"Why?"

"The money thing is going great, but I'm interested in getting a"—she hesitated long enough to make sure she didn't sound desperate—"a boyfriend."

Quita turned around then. "That's right. I promised you a plan, and I've got one."

Jimmy angled his chair at their table and Quita's look of disbelief didn't deter him a bit. He seemed flattered by her annoyance.

"You are too bold," she said to him. "Can you give us some privacy?"

"You came here to talk to your girlfriends?"

"Yes." When he didn't back off, he gained another minute of her attention. "Order us another round and when I'm done, we'll talk."

A staring contest ensued before he did as she asked. The promise of intimacy hung in the air between them.

"I want that kind of power," Ebony told BJ.

BJ couldn't lie. She wanted it, too. "You're drunk, Eb."

"I have a hollow leg. I can hold my liquor better than most people. As long as we've been friends, you should know that by now," she said, defensive.

Quita and BJ burst out laughing. Ebony wasn't a big talker and when she did, she was never drunk. This was a night of firsts.

"Well, if y'all are serious, I've got an idea." Quita finished her drink, and before her glass hit the table, another was delivered. "Let's make a pact to have at least one date a week with a man."

"If I can't get a date now, how will I get one once a week?" Ebony wanted to know.

Quita gazed at her. "It's the law of averages, Ebony. Men are looking at you right now. But are you paying attention? No. You're shoving your face with potato skins and chicken fingers and talking to me."

Ebony quit eating and canvassed the room.

"They're looking this way, but there're fifty women over here."

"Damn, Ebony. If you're not going to try, that's on you," Quita told her. "But I've got goals, and so does BJ. So how about it?"

"How will it work?" BJ wanted to know, although inside she knew she'd agree. She always worked better with a goal.

"The rules are simple. We each have to have one date a week with a man, and to keep us honest, we'd have our own date night, just us girls."

"Can a date be over coffee?" Ebony asked, tilting a little and wearing a goofy grin.

"Any date, Ebony," Quita said, her eyes bright as Jimmy started back, his hands full.

"Want to have date night on Sunday when we have our investment club meetings?" BJ offered, trying to plan her next three dates.

"Yeah," they both agreed.

The guitarist gestured toward BJ. If she got lucky, this game was the jump-start she needed.

"What's going to keep one of us from backing out?" BJ asked.

"Make it worth money," Ebony offered.

Quita lifted her glass. "I'm willing to stake my investment in the club."

Two thousand dollars' worth of silence hung between them.

BJ was sure that, overall, she had the most money out of the three, but it wasn't like she could afford to lose a couple thousand dollars. But, she reasoned, she'd spend that much on something else if she wanted it bad enough. "I'm in."

All eyes were on Ebony.

"I'm in, too. In fact," Ebony picked up her large purse and pulled a small memo pad from inside. "We need a contract. Then there's no question about what was said and what we agreed to."

BJ didn't hesitate to sign the paper, nor did the others.

Quita turned to Jimmy and ran her finger from one of his shoulders to the other. "You finally ready to pay attention to me?"

She stood. "Dance with me."

The two moved onto the empty dance floor.

BJ wished she had the magic touch. But this game was only in the first quarter. Her stomach ached at the idea that she could lose, but then again, this would give her incentive to pursue dating seriously.

The band played the last chords before walking off the stage. BJ made her way toward the guitarist.

A throng of women stood between them, vying for his attention. He was nice to them, but he telegraphed a message that he was aware of her and that soon he'd give her his full attention.

Another woman in this situation might have gotten annoyed, but BJ didn't. She'd straddled the same fence of fame.

"I love tall women," he said, once he got close.

"I like a man who knows what to do with a tall woman."

His million-dollar smile invited her in. "I'd like to buy you a drink. That okay with you, Squirt?"

BJ got an attitude, although she couldn't stop smiling. "I hope there're no more tall jokes in you're repertoire."

He got a little closer. "What should I call you, then?"

In all of her life, BJ had never been called Squirt. She liked it. "BJ, to my friends."

He clasped her palm in his rough-hewn hand. "Hello, BJ."

"What's your name?"

He conferred with the bartender and got himself an ice water and her a raspberry martini. The only way he could've known that was her drink was if he'd been paying attention from the stage. A tingle skated up her spine. When he finished his ice water he wrapped her waist with his hands and started slow dancing. "My name is Mike. But you can call me Big Squirt."

A chuckle rumbled up his chest as she gave him an "Are you for real?" look.

Then she felt his big squirter.

She didn't want to act giddy, but she wasn't far from it.

His hands possessed her and kept her where he wanted her to be.

BJ looked over to their table and was shocked to see Ebony talking to the same man who'd approached her earlier. The girl was even smiling.

Jimmy had his face so close to Quita's they may as well have been kissing.

Success already.

Date night was going to change their lives forever.

Chapter 3
Ebony

Ebony unlocked the door of the Braeden Construction and Supplies corporate office and scooted into the coolness. The temperature outside had soared to a sweat-breaking eighty-five degrees, no clouds or rain in sight. She wished she'd worn layers, then she could regulate her body temperature by peeling them off as needed, but the thin silk blouse and suit jacket would have to do for today.

She turned off the security system and entered her cubicle outside her boss's office, shrugged out of her jacket, and dropped her briefcase.

Business casual hadn't yet become the norm for her, although Stan dressed in stain-resistant chinos and a short-sleeve polo shirt.

Ebony sat down, her stockings hissing as she crossed her legs, and opened her briefcase.

The business card from the guy she'd met at Taboo fell out.

Grabbing it and the handwritten agreement they'd all signed for date night, she shoved them into her desk. BJ and Quita had left the club with grins on their faces, while she'd left with the receipt from her drink and appetizers.

Her "friend" Wes hadn't offered to buy her a drink. He'd given her his card, *before* she'd refused his generous offer for an evening at the Hampton Inn. At first she'd been offended, but he'd made her laugh, and on a Friday night when everyone else was getting action, that mattered.

She pulled out the card and studied it. Maybe he'd lost her number. Quita said it was a numbers game. Maybe she needed to make the second move. As she dialed, she held her breath. The disruption signal sounded. *"The number you have reached has been disconnected."*

Deflated, Ebony jammed the card into the shredder and pulled the overnight orders off the fax machine. She had all this work to process and no time to wonder why she, again, wasn't the chosen one. Work had been her savior before, and by the looks of things, Stan wasn't going to let up on loading her down with responsibility.

She pulled the letter to Leah Waverly from her case.

While she was busy being the VP of his personal affairs, office trysts, and intermittent dalliances, he was out screwing around. What she knew about him could wreck his suburban life and cause him to have to lay off a manager to be able to afford spousal support.

The name Leah Waverly stared back in Stan's chicken scratch, the outline of a check visible through the envelope. Who was this woman, and why was Stan so dim?

Ebony booted up the system and tapped into the company's personnel files, but Leah Waverly's name never appeared. *Must have been up to his old tricks again,* using temp agencies as dating services. He had to be playing around on Penney, his wife of five years, because he never handled his own correspondence. He couldn't spell worth a damn.

She pulled another company envelope and letter opener from her drawer and slit the addressed envelope open. Her fingers were on the check when the outside door jangled.

Stan was early.

He appeared around the cubicle just as she let the papers drift to the floor beneath her desk.

"Morning, Ebony. Did you get that letter out yesterday?" He dropped his Palm Pilot into the in-box and flipped over the blank envelope.

Her heart pounded her unflappable smile into place. "Good morning, and yes. Did you need me to follow up on it or something?" she asked, fishing.

"No." He looked relieved as he walked away, whistling. She brought air into her lungs but it caught in her throat as he turned back. "I need this." He took the envelope from her desk and walked into his office.

"No problem. I've got more."

Ebony squeezed her thighs and tried to control her shaking. That was too close.

The check and letter were faceup on the chair pad. She scooped them up and shoved them inside the waistband of her stockings, flat against her belly. How would she get rid of them now?

Who had she thought she was? One of Charlie's Angels? In the past, Stan hadn't gone to too much trouble to hide his affairs, so maybe she was off base. But he still had grounds to fire her if he ever found out she'd opened his personal correspondence.

She'd have to find a moment to sneak down to the mailbox without him knowing. Ebony forced herself to go about her normal duties, but kept hitting the wrong keys as she checked the Internet orders. She swore under her breath.

"Ebony, are you all right out there?"

"Fine!"

"Somebody needs a break. I don't know about you, but I could use a cup of coffee. Feel up to walking down to Starbucks?"

Relief hit her square in the chest. The mailbox was right past the coffee shop. "Sure," she said in a nicer voice. "Be back in a few."

As she fingered a five from her wallet, her fortune from last night's Chinese dinner slid halfway out. *Today's correspondence affects all your tomorrows.*

She resisted touching her bellyful of dynamite.

As she walked out, she slipped into the copy room, copied the papers, and folded them in half before securing them beneath her skirt again.

Sitting down with their coffees on a tray, Ebony discreetly unfolded the letter and started reading. Stan *was* cheating, and now he had an heir. Something his union with Penney had never reaped. There would be hell to pay if she ever found out.

Ebony became aware of the presence of a man over her shoulder. She almost scalded herself trying to conceal the note, and turned to get at look at him.

Hefty, and dressed awkwardly in a department-store business suit and shoes, he was definitely blue collar. His apologetic smile sufficed and Ebony turned around. He was okay looking, but if she had a type, she wanted her man to be white collar. With the exception of her brief encounter Friday night, she hadn't had a date in thirteen months. Perhaps her prototype needed a face-lift. She tried to adopt a friendly attitude as she looked at him. "Hi." Ebony cringed. *How lame.*

Quita ignored men and they turned to cream, and BJ mentioned that she'd been in the WNBA, and the conversation wouldn't end for hours.

But let Ebony say "hi," and men yawned and eyed their watches.

Much to her surprise, the slightly rumpled man sat next to her. "Do you mind?"

She scooted the carton of coffees over.

"I'm a little nervous. I've got an interview." He held a napkin under his chin and sipped his coffee. "I know I look strange with this napkin, but if I blow this interview because of a coffee stain on my shirt, I'll never forgive myself."

She sighed, relieved. "What are you going for?"

"Manager of a distribution center."

There were dozens of those in this industrial park in Norcross. She worked in one, in fact.

She sized him up as a potential date.

He didn't look bad. Taller than her five one by about six inches, he was thick and strong looking. Maybe they could get to know one another. "What's your name?" Ebony asked.

"Boyle Robinson. Yours?"

Aw, hell.

"I'm Ebony Manchester," she added reluctantly.

"Pretty name for a pretty lady."

"Thank you." The adage of "don't judge a book by its cover" entered her mind, and she pushed aside her prejudice.

"Do you work around here?" Boyle said, drinking carefully.

Whoa. She didn't need a stalker on her hands. "Not really," she replied, taking creative license with her interpretation. "Live nearby?" This time it was he who hesitated.

His name was Boyle, for God's sake. He certainly didn't think she wanted something from him, did he?

Ebony gathered the coffee and condiments and started toward the door. "I'm not trying to pick you up. I was just making conversation," she said, and walked into the sunshine.

Her mother's favorite put-downs swam through her head and Ebony zeroed in on the one about her not deserving a man, and agreed. Not even one named Boyle.

The bells from the coffee shop caught in the wind as the door closed, but Ebony didn't break her stride.

"Hey, Ebony!"

She walked faster as she heard Boyle panting behind her.

She rounded on him and removed the lid from Stan's coffee cup. If Boyle tried anything, he'd be thinking about Al Green for the rest of the day in Grady Memorial Hospital burn unit. "Back off, if you know what's good for you."

Slowly he raised the copies of Stan's letter. "You forgot these."

Shock and embarrassment burned in her stomach. "I'm sorry."

"I heard the ladies in Atlanta were crazy."

He placed the papers on the hood of the nearest car and hurried back the way he'd come.

"I wouldn't have—really," she said, but gave up. She dropped the troublesome letter inside the mailbox, concealed the others, and trudged back to work.

An image of her mother filled her mind, only it was herself as an unhappy woman, too mean to see that she'd ruined her own life. Ebony began whispering reassurance to herself. *I'm a good person. I'm a good person. I'm a good person.*

The phone rang and she dragged on her headset. "Braeden Construction, how may I assist you?"

"Eb, it's Quita."

"What can I do for you?"

"Stop being so formal, fool, I've seen you drunk."

Quita could be so unnerving. "Marquita, what do you want?"

"Come to the club tonight for drinks. I want you to meet someone."

Ebony's heart thumped at the possibility. "Who?"

"Don't worry about it. Just say you're coming."

Ebony wanted their dating game to be successful, but her natural suspicion piqued. "Did you invite BJ?"

"No. Look, I gotta go."

"Why not?"

"Because," Quita sounded impatient, "this man wants a short woman and you fit the bill. Happy?"

"Thanks, but no thanks." Was that all she was? Short?

A third to a group where Quita already had a date and she was doing a favor for her date's cousin Mookmook?

She might not be a lot of things, but Ebony had standards. "I have laundry to wash tonight, Quita. No thanks."

"Eb, tell me you have a date, and I'll leave you alone." Quita hesitated half a second. "Well?"

Was there ever a time when Quita took no for an answer? Ebony couldn't escape the fact that there was nothing at home but her evil mother and lazy aunt.

"Who's paying?" Ebony asked, stalling.

"Damn, I'll pay if it's like that. Are you coming?"

The last three days of meeting men played in her mind. She was 0 for 2. Maybe this guy would be her knight in shining armor. Then she'd leave her unhappy mother forever. "What time should I be there?"

"Seven-thirty. See you then."

Ebony settled down to work and prayed that God was truly merciful and her date tonight wasn't with Boyle Robinson.

Chapter 4

Quita

Marquita moved through Upscale, the restaurant and club she co-owned with silent partners, spotting little imperfections and correcting them.

Customers didn't know of her desire to make their dining existence an on-earth utopia, but found her attention to the finer details graceful and charming. Her waitstaff loved when she hit the floor each day to greet customers and make everyone feel welcome. When Quita was there, tips were larger and everyone left happy.

She approached a table where servers were resetting for the next guests. She gathered up all the sterling silverware and her staff froze.

"Take these into the kitchen and have Mack rewash them by hand."

Carmella, top hostess for the restaurant, shook out a clean maroon napkin and accepted the silver. She'd been with Quita long enough to not question her judgment.

"What's wrong with those? I just got them from the kitchen," Salvo, the youngest and newest member of the waitstaff said, irritated. The table was his and if it wasn't set, he wouldn't get the next large seating. Or the superb tip it promised.

She looked at the red-nosed young man. "Come with me, Salvo. Everyone, please resume your duties."

The waiter for the patio took the iced teapot that Salvo had been about to serve and headed to the kitchen. He would dispose of it properly.

"How are you feeling today?"

"Fine, Ms. Snell. I don't understand why you sent back the silverware. A party of eight is waiting."

Inside her office, she looked at the closed-circuit monitors and saw the very group that Salvo spoke of being seated and given complimentary beverages.

"You don't look fine," she told him.

Salvo wiped his hands on his black pants and tried not to look so sick. "Ma'am, I am. Can I get back to work now?"

"Not today. You have the flu. One of the staff saw you sneeze on the silverware you were setting the table with, and over the iced tea. That, in and of itself, could get you dismissed."

Eyes wide, he coughed and tried to dispel the truth, but she held up her hand. "You're clearly not at one hundred percent. Or else those details wouldn't have been neglected."

He felt his own forehead and rolled his eyes. "I have to work or I won't be able to pay my bills."

"I understand that, but you can't work here sick and infect the customers. Your summer flu could put me out of business. Go home. Come back Monday when you're better."

Salvo stood in front of her desk like a disappointed child. He turned slowly and walked toward the door. "If I'm better by Wednesday, can I come back?"

She couldn't help but feel sorry for him. "Yes, but with a doctor's note. Otherwise, Monday."

The door slammed shut and Quita was out of her chair but stopped herself from going after him by counting to ten.

Maybe he didn't realize he'd slammed the door. She'd give him the benefit of the doubt, this time. But let him slam another door, and his ass would be on the sidewalk.

She sat down and her gaze slid to the mirror she'd forgotten to put away before her shift started. Guarded green-brown eyes reflected back as black hair flipped and dipped in a mass of waves, ending below her shoulders. Normally she wore it clipped back, but the barrette had broken after she'd arrived at work and she'd had to go loose and natural. People often misjudged her, thinking her fair skin and beauty were a pass for a lack of intelligence.

But her Martinique-born grandmother Mimi had taught Quita about the strong woman who didn't have to rely on a man for anything. Mimi had loved Pappy unconditionally. Their loving union bore five daughters, yet ended when Pappy declared another woman his wife and left Mimi. Heartbroken until his death in '89, Mimi turned over a new leaf and raised hell with men until her death in '99.

When Quita's half-black, half island-born mother had lain down with Quita's Jamaican father, their child's fiery spirit had been all but written in stone.

Mimi and Pappy's daughters had struck out to find love and had ten daughters between them. Of the ten, the first four girls had been created in the name of love. The next four had been a cry for proof that love existed, and the last two as good-bye to a dream.

Now Quita's mother and aunts were bitter, broken women who hated men as much as they hated having been fooled by them.

Their years of disappointment had been tossed like broken sticks at Quita's feet, and like a loyal warrior princess, she'd made shoes and trudged into adulthood. In thirty years she'd taken no prisoners, but that hadn't stopped her from needing the only thing a man could give her. His sperm. And not just any donation. She wanted a baby born from love.

How could she want the one thing she'd been taught didn't exist? *Manhater, seeking man to love.* She shook her head at the irony.

She had the empire. Maybe this would have to be her lifelong baby. The phone beeped.

"Marquita Snell," she answered.

"Ms. Snell, this is Cori from Dr. Tate's office."

It was seven o'clock. Late for a doctor. "Yes, Cori. What can I do for you?"

"Dr. Tate wants you to come in so she can discuss the results of your annual exam."

"Was there a problem?"

"She'll go over all the results with you. Can you come in next Monday at eight-thirty?"

Dread hit her first in the stomach, then fear. "Of course. I'll be there."

Chapter 5
Ebony

The atmosphere in the club sizzled with sexual tension as men walked around eyeing the houseful of single ladies. There were two women for every one man, and though it was obvious this was just a friendly competition, only the best female would leave with a phone number, or better, a man.

Ebony waited at the bar for Quita and assessed her fellow sisters. If this crowd was a snapshot of the male psyche, men liked fit women who didn't mind struttin' their stuff in high heels, short skirts, coy smiles, long hair—with their own money.

After all, drinks at Upscale weren't cheap, but made up for the price with potency.

The girls who didn't make the cut lined the walls, pointing out the women they were jealous of.

Ebony tried not to engage in the envious people watching, but couldn't help but compare her clothes, hairstyle, and confidence level against the women who'd capture the prize of the night: the men.

How did these women manage to look so put together so soon after work? What kinds of jobs did they have that allowed them to buy expensive clothes *and* drive the luxury cars that lined the valet parking lot?

Ebony had parked in the supermarket lot across the street, and had braved crossing the busy intersection to get to the club. And now that she was here, she was ready to meet her date for the evening.

A woman in spiked heels and a sheer shirt sauntered toward her and Ebony sat back on her bar stool, her back pressed into the teak. The woman had circled the room ten minutes ago, looking for a place to roost, but Ebony wasn't going to give up her spot. Then she'd be like the women on the wall, and she'd suffered enough blows to the ego for one day.

"Excuse me." The woman smelled of Gucci Envy perfume, worth every penny of its eighty-five-dollar-an-ounce asking price. She squeezed in, her body moving Ebony aside as she wiggled her fingers to get the bartender's attention. "Hey, sweetie. Rum and Coke."

Ebony sat at an angle, waiting for the woman to move, but couldn't believe it when the gold-sprinkled statue turned around, spread her elbows, and leaned back, staking her claim on Ebony's space.

No this bitch didn't.

At this rate, Ebony would have to get up and move her stool just to have a little breathing room, and in the process, lose more ground to this vulture.

"I was sitting here," Ebony told her.

The woman eyed the space she'd just stolen. "Far as I can see, you're still sitting. So—" She turned with a smirk on her face. "Hey," she called to three ladies and waved them over. "I've got room right here."

They crowded in, oblivious to Ebony. "I hope I'm not in your way," she said sarcastically.

Two of the women looked down their surgically perfected noses. "Please. Could you be more invisible?"

Ebony turned away from their smug dismissal.

She hated this type of women. Had since high school. They were the cheerleaders who dated football players, while she was in the band and didn't date at all.

While they were platinum filled, she was faux silver.

She tried to uncross her legs so she could leave, when her jacket slipped off the back of her chair. She saw the Kathie Lee Gifford label when they did.

Laughter resounded around her, punctuated by little yelps and screams.

Humiliation raced through her veins. Any other day, she was a proud shopper at Wal-Mart, but not today. Not here.

She grabbed her jacket and hurried into the ladies room.

Inside the locked stall, she sat on the toilet, her hands over her face. Why had she let them get the best of her?

All her life she'd been putting women like that in their place. But lately, she'd been off her mark. She bought cheap clothes, because clothes weren't as important as buying a house for herself. She'd made the mistake of taking her mother in after she'd had knee surgery. That had been two years ago, and her mother was still "recovering." Then Aunt Jo had come to help her mother, and never left.

Between their medical bills, prescriptions, and personal needs, they'd run through almost twelve thousand dollars of her money.

Ebony shook her head. Her entire savings to buy her dream house was now gone. And two days ago, her mother had asked when Ebony would get her next raise. She wanted to replace Ebony's tacky old sofa.

The outer door to the bathroom opened and two women entered, talking. "You can be such a bitch. That lady was sitting there first. You don't have the right to bully people, Leslie."

"But now she's not. What's your problem? I found us a space, didn't I?"

Ebony raised her sensible shoes and planted them softly on the door.

"Yeah, but you can't keep running people over like you rule the world. I'm going home. I'm tired."

"I can't believe you." Leslie laughed. "You're leaving because I chased some homely woman away from the bar? Be for real."

"God, Les, that was me a couple years ago."

"Short, no-makeup-wearing, nappy-headed, and dressed in cheap clothes," Leslie said in disbelief. "That was never you. If it were, you wouldn't be my friend."

Ebony's face stung and her legs shook.

The bathroom door banged open. "Were you at the bar a few minutes ago?" Marquita's voice rang out angrily.

"Yeah. Why?"

"Get out of my club and don't ever come back."

"*Your* club?"

Ebony came out of the stall.

"This is my club and that is my best friend," Quita declared. "You'd better think twice before you and your friends insult someone else. Now get out."

"She wasn't one of them." Ebony pointed to the woman who'd defended her.

"No, but I'm going anyway."

"You're welcome to come back anytime," Quita told her.

The woman gave Quita a small smile. "Thanks," she said and left.

The other woman finished touching up her hair and turned around. "I don't want to stay in this hick bar anyway. It isn't the caliber crowd I'm looking for."

Quita opened the door. "Rocky," she called to the man Ebony always thought of as a truck. "Put this trash on the curb."

The woman tried to get indignant, but Rocky took her by the arm and ushered her out of the ladies room.

"You shouldn't ever let people push you around."

Quita was still shouting, her eyes dangerously bright. She looked

30

ready to fight. Ebony couldn't believe what just happened. In her whole life no one had ever taken up for her.

"I was caught off guard. You saw everything on the monitors in your office?"

Quita nodded.

"Everything okay, Quita?"

"Just dandy, now that I've kicked the mayor's niece out."

"You can't be serious! Won't you get in trouble for that?"

"Could if I'd busted a cap in her ass like I wanted to, but no. The mayor and me have an understanding. He doesn't tell me how to run this place, and I don't tell him how to run the city. Except when it comes to picking up the garbage or raising taxes. Then he knows to expect my call."

Quita turned toward the mirror and exhaled a loud breath. Calmer, she took a few more.

Ebony didn't even bother to look at herself. "Quita, where've you been? I thought we were meeting at seven?"

"Dealing with some work stuff. It's over now, so let's go."

The sting of the woman's words still haunted Ebony. She'd never been a princess, but homely?

"Can I ask you something?"

"Shoot," Quita said, fluffing her silky curls.

"Am I homely?"

"Bitches like that are right only to themselves. Ignore them."

Ebony stared at herself in the mirror and saw the same plain face she'd seen every day of her life.

"What she thinks doesn't matter, Ebony. It's what you think of yourself. If you think you need more makeup, get some. Different clothes, buy some. But don't give them power over you. Got it?"

Quita spoke with such passion, Ebony started to believe her. She felt light for the first time that day. "I like having friends of influence."

"Good. Then get your happy ass out of the bathroom and let's go have some fun."

* * *

Late that night, Ebony unearthed her diary from the locked suitcase she kept in the back of her closet, away from prying eyes. She sat on her bed with the light shining on the lined page.

> *Today started out rough. Stan's infidelity has come back to haunt him and one day might ruin his marriage. I can't believe I read his mail, but it's a shame when your married boss's extramarital love life is more exciting than your single one. In a way I feel pathetic, especially after the incident with Boyle Robinson and the women at the club. And my date tonight . . .*
> *Terran Neville was a nice man. But he didn't ask for my number. He didn't try to kiss me or even shake my hand. He patted me on my elbow in that "we're friends" kind of way. But we're not. Diary, am I ugly?*

Ebony looked into her dresser mirror.

> *Should I change my hair? I've been doing home perms to save money and my hair doesn't have that polished professional look other Atlanta women have, but you know why I've been doing this. Every night I pray for God to send me someone who will love me unconditionally, yet I'm still waiting. It's been thirty-one years, one hundred twenty days, and I can't help but wonder if tomorrow will be any different.*

Ebony sighed and scratched out the last line. All the self-help books she had on her shelves discouraged this type of negative thinking.

She took a deep breath and gathered her courage.

> *Dear Lord, I'm ready whenever you are. Even tomorrow. Hint, hint.*

Chapter 6

BJ

BJ set the stock reports, financial section from the newspaper, and a vase of yellow roses on the table before going into the kitchen for the fresh fruit and mimosas.

Today was their first official date night, and she was excited to hear about everyone's week. But they had this investment-club business to handle first. This meeting marked a milestone. They'd made money four weeks in a row. This past week by far had been the most profitable.

BJ knew both Quita and Ebony thought she was hiding big bank from her years in the WNBA, and she did have a retirement account she couldn't touch until she was sixty-five. But not much else.

Besides her current salary that went to her monthly bills, and a few extras, she needed this money as much as they did.

The retirement village her grandmother lived in necessitated BJ's continued success. Thank God two years ago she'd paid ahead, but with the increase in fees for this year, she'd have to do something to generate more income. She grabbed the phone, hit the number two, and hurried up the stairs.

"Granny, it's BJ. How are you?"

"I'm still here, so I guess I'm doing fine."

BJ laughed at her grandmother's wit. "You go to chapel today?"

"Yes, but they don't sing like in the Baptist Church. I'm gone need some more church music for my stereo."

BJ stepped into her closet, one of her most favorite places in the whole house. One wall had been designed with trim built-in drawers made from pink glass.

"You learned how to work your CD player? That's good news."

Granny laughed. "No, that doohickey is too complicated. I just get Amos, that young orderly, to put it in and I unplug it when I want it off."

"That's not very modern, Granny. I signed you up for the simple electronics class up there. Why haven't you gone?"

"My method don't require much training. Why waste my time? Oh, there's Isabel. I'd better go. Bye, sweet granddaughter."

"I love you, Granny. I'll see you next week."

"Okay." Granny hung up and BJ shimmied into a white sundress and flat beige sandals. She still subscribed to the school that women with big feet didn't wear white sandals.

Good. Granny was fine and she was dressed.

Relieved, BJ dug out the number of the man who'd occupied her thoughts for about ten hours and dialed. "Hey, Mike, BJ. How are you?"

"Hey, baby," he said, groggily.

"You're not up yet?" It was almost noon. Maybe he'd found another two-legged reason to stay in bed, since she'd declined his offer last night. They'd been out twice since meeting a week ago, but insecurity crawled through her. Mike had a wandering eye. When they'd been together, he was quick to smile at other women. But he'd bestowed those same charming qualities on her. How could she make him focus all his attention on her? "I'll let you go."

"I can talk to you," Mike said. "Why don't you come over and see me?"

She flushed hot. "I don't think so."

"I'm glad you called. Want me to come see you? We could snuggle up together and watch a movie."

BJ sighed. This wasn't going the way she'd expected. She'd just met him and now he wanted to get into bed? "I can't talk long. I just wondered if you wanted to do something later?"

"You know what I want to do—" He started talking to someone else in the background, and BJ strained to hear. "Just a minute, BJ," he said.

Why didn't he get off the phone if he had company? She didn't share. "Hello," she said, and got no response. "Hey!"

"Hmm?" he said.

"Why didn't you say you had company? I'll talk to you another time."

"No, baby. That was my niece. Why don't you let me come over and make you feel good?"

His niece? And he expected her to buy that? To a musician, women were a dime a dozen.

"BJ, you there?" The woman in the background wasn't going off on him. Maybe that had been his niece. "I'm still here. Look, I've got company arriving soon, so I'd better go."

"Another man?"

"Some girlfriends."

"I like girlfriends." He chuckled. "Do you want me to cook for you and your girlfriends?"

She giggled, too, and sighed. Maybe she was just paranoid. He sounded so sexy. "No, we can feed ourselves." Just slow the conversation down; don't talk about him coming over here, or her going over there, but get to know one another. The doorbell rang. "I've got to go. I'll call you later."

"You want to meet at Colony Square for lunch tomorrow?" he asked.

His invitation squashed her uncertainties. "Twelve-thirty, south entrance. Bye," she said, and was glad to cradle the phone before she hurried through the foyer to the front door and pulled it open. "Hey," she greeted Ebony and Quita.

"Hey, girl, are we rich yet?" Quita asked the same question before every meeting as she led the way to the kitchen.

"Not quite, but we're getting there. Come on in."

"What you got to drink?"

"Didn't get enough last night?" BJ asked, then regretted the reference.

"You two went out last night?" Offended, Ebony dropped her bag on the chair.

BJ knew better than to give too many details. "I ended up at the club with a client before Quita left for the night."

"Oh." The curt word said more than it didn't. Ebony was hurt. She always was. But the truth was that Quita knew how to have a good time, and Ebony overanalyzed everything until fun got up and ran away.

"Was your client your date?" Ebony quizzed.

"Yes. Nothing to brag about, but I'm cautiously optimistic. Anybody hungry? I've got everything set out for omelets."

BJ moved on so that Ebony wouldn't belabor the point. Meeting Troy out last night had been a fluke. She'd been watching a game with a couple of old basketball friends at ESPN Zone downtown, and he had come in. They'd ended up hanging out, and had gone to Upscale to end the evening.

Troy had tried to come home with her, but she wasn't having it. Even after retiring from the Celtics five years ago, he was still a ladies' man. But he had a nice personality, and he knew how to take no for an answer and not be offended.

"Do you think he'd like to go out with you again?"

This time BJ was offended. "I don't know if *I* want to go out with *him* again."

Quita poured a mimosa and took a cautious sip. "You got OJ straight up?"

BJ drew her hands back from the warm French rolls.

"What's wrong with you?" Ebony demanded.

"Nothing. Can't I wait until a decent hour before I start drinking?"

"You never have before," Ebony pointed out, much to Quita's chagrin. "It's almost twelve anyway. I'm making my omelet first," she called as if she were a child.

Quita's cheeks flamed, and she bent over and adjusted the strap on her heels before she dropped her portfolio onto the chair. "Go ahead, with your silly-behind self."

"Fine, you go, if you're going to get an attitude," Ebony said defensively.

Quita got situated on the barstool and removed her sunglasses. "No, 'cause I'm not dealing with your sour mood all day because you didn't get to make your food first."

"Quita," BJ said, changing the contentious direction of the conversation. "Why don't you read our status reports. I think all four are beside your plate."

Quita took her time, undecided. BJ silently begged her to back down. "All right. On EXS, the pharmaceutical company, our initial investment was seven dollars a share. We bought fifty, and it's trading at fifteen eighty-three."

Everybody cooked their omelets and then moved to the enclosed patio and ate there.

"How did we do for the week?"

Quita finished and BJ read from the treasurer's report. "Eight thousand, one hundred forty-five dollars."

Ebony stopped chewing to review her paperwork. "That's two thousand fifteen dollars a piece. What's next? Are the sell orders in?"

"They're in, but do we want to hold anything?" BJ asked. "Three stocks haven't reached the sell level."

"Do you think they will?"

"We can hold for another week," Quita suggested. "But if they drop more than a dollar, we sell immediately. Agreed?"

The other two nodded. "Great," Quita said.

By the time they'd finished their omelets, they'd decided on four new stocks to purchase, and BJ collected their hundred-dollar checks.

"I'll put in the buy order and send a confirmation when the broker gets back to me." Quita gathered her things.

"Where are you going?"

"I've got errands to run, Ebony, if you must know."

"Today is date night. I thought we were supposed to have a recap. Did you meet someone?" Ebony quizzed.

The blank expression on Quita's face said more than if she'd cracked a joke. "Yes, and you met him the night we doubled."

Ebony chewed slowly, thinking back.

"Give up his statistics," BJ said.

Quita balanced her portfolio on her knees. "His name is Richard, he's thirty-six and single. He's divorced and has three children who sometimes live at home. But, he's not the man for me. So the search continues."

"Why? He was all over you."

Ebony didn't understand Quita the way she did, BJ thought. Quita wasn't a woman who wanted a man to give her everything. She was a hunter. If the capture was too easy, she lost interest.

"And?" Quita quipped.

Ebony looked to BJ for help. "And what do you want from him?"

"I want someone who knows how to take care of himself and his business, professional and personal. I want someone who's independent and self-assured. Someone who can keep up with me, and satisfy me in bed."

"You only met this guy, what, two times, so how would you know he's incapable of giving you those things?" Ebony asked.

"I know." Quita loaded her plate in the dishwasher.

"*How* do you know?" BJ asked, restocking the refrigerator with food. She suddenly stood upright. "You didn't."

"What?" Ebony jumped in.

38

"She slept with him," BJ said.

Quita smirked. "We didn't sleep."

"Hmmp. I could never do that." Ebony shook her church hairdo hard.

"That's the difference between me and you. I'm not waiting around to see two years from now if we're compatible. I want to know the important stuff up front. Saves time on the back end."

"Sex confuses things, Quita. You know that," Ebony advised, giving Quita her "I know best" glare.

"Okay, then," Quita said, entertaining Ebony. "When was the last time you were confused?"

"That has nothing to do with anything."

"Sure it does. I'm challenging your hypothesis. What proof do you have that it's better not to have sex first? You met Terran. He was a nice man. Are you going to see him again?"

"No. But that's not because we didn't have sex. We didn't have anything in common."

"Girls, this is getting off track," BJ said, but was swept aside.

"He's in marketing, white collar, fit, and somewhat handsome, if you like a man with a moustache. What more are you looking for?" Quita demanded.

Ebony fidgeted. "He practices some type of religion I've never heard of."

"So?"

"I don't want to start something when I know it's important that the man I want is a Christian."

"But he was nice and charming and all the other things, right?"

"Yes, but—"

Quita unfolded her sunglasses. "That's my point. You used your discretion to rule out a man who has many qualities you found appealing, but once you heard he didn't have one thing," she snapped her fingers, "gone."

"Sex isn't a quality!" Ebony argued.

"Let me finish," Quita said. "He lacked something important

and you decided not to give him a shot. How is what I did any different?"

"Because sex is sex! It's"—Ebony struggled—"invasive and physical and revealing. All I did was have a conversation, dinner, a pat on the arm, and good night. My evening was over."

"And mine ended a few hours later."

"But it's dangerous."

BJ felt sorry for Ebony. She and Quita had had this conversation many times before. But trying to convince Quita was like changing the direction of flowing lava.

"I use protection. Nobody is going to kill me."

"Don't count on it." Ebony went to the sink and started the water.

"Ebony, I merely accelerated the inevitable. I don't have time to waste."

Quita shoved on her sunglasses, hurried up behind Ebony, and kissed her on the cheek. "We cool?"

Ebony grabbed her hand. "Always. Just be careful. Hey, have y'all ever been to Gigolo Dancer night at the X-tasy?"

Both stared at her.

"I've been to clubs like that, but not that one specifically. Why?" Quita asked slyly.

"I'm just asking." Ebony looked like she wanted to hide.

"When is it?" Quita asked, consulting her Palm Pilot. BJ did the same.

"Tuesday or Wednesday. You free?"

"I am," BJ said.

"Me, too. Okay, we're on. Let's meet there. I'll have to go back to work afterwards. BJ, walk me out."

BJ and Quita strolled to the front door and Quita urged BJ out with a head nod.

"What's up?"

"I've got an ob-gyn appointment tomorrow."

"What's wrong?" BJ kept her voice low.

"Nothing that I know of, but she usually just refills my pills and I see her the next year. But this time—"

That's why she hadn't drunk the mimosas.

"I'll go with you." BJ pulled the door closed a little farther.

"No, I don't want you to go. I just want you to be there if I need to talk."

"Okay." BJ tried to keep the hurt to herself. Quita was so independent. But sometimes she reminded BJ of a thick oak tree all by itself in the pasture. Every now and then, she needed someone to lean on. "When will you call me?"

"Tomorrow night. Don't tell Ebony. I don't want to hear from the mass choir any more this week." She sucked her cheeks in. "I don't mean that."

"I know."

BJ was careful not to look at Quita. She'd already seen discomfort. She didn't want to see fear. She wanted to ask more questions, but Quita was funny about her business. Everything about Quita was on a need-to-know basis. BJ could argue the point, but she wouldn't win.

Quita kept her gaze locked on her Kelly green Mercedes and so did BJ. "It's probably nothing, so there's no need to talk about it."

"Okay," BJ said softly.

"Okay." Quita got into her car and drove away.

Chapter 7
Quita

"Marquita, fibroid tumors are growing on the inside and outside of your uterus." Doctor Ann Tate pointed to the shadowy ultrasound film.

Before shock settled into her brain, Quita began firing questions. "Are they cancerous?"

"No, but eventually, they'll have to be removed. This is one reason why your cycle is so heavy, and the reason for the bad cramping."

Quita suddenly wished she'd taken another Xanax. She needed a bigger buffer to absorb the shock. "I wouldn't be pregnant by any chance, would I?"

The doctor placed the results on the desk. "Have you been trying?"

"Every chance I get."

She shook her head. "No, I'm sorry, you're not."

Quita tried but couldn't contain her disappointment. "Will the fibroids prevent me from getting pregnant?"

"There's a bigger issue here."

Breath burst from her mouth. *Damn.* "What is it, then?"

"It's highly unlikely that you will ever get pregnant the conventional way."

"W-what?" She felt as if the doctor had placed a gun to her stomach and pulled the trigger.

How many men had she been with over the past year? Twenty? Thirty? Every time she'd seduced one, she'd prayed he would have swimmers strong enough to defy her stubborn body. But no, the number of men had nothing to do with biology.

"You have endometriosis. I'm sorry."

Quita walked around the office, searching for answers, searching for someone to blame. "So that's it. I'm barren? What—" *Good am I*, she wanted to say. "Why can't I? I'm only thirty. I'm young, healthy. I take care of myself." She hiccupped back the lump in her throat, but that didn't stop tears from burning her cheeks.

She'd done everything right. Hadn't had a kid young. Had gotten her education and followed the unwritten protocol for matriculation from the multicolored walls of Philly, to the white walls of corporate America. She'd been one of life's perfect students. So how had she failed the class?

"I have to have a baby. That's all I've ever wanted." She finally vocalized the wish she'd kept secret for twenty years.

"Marquita, come on. Sit down."

Dr. Tate came around her desk and guided Quita back to her seat and sat beside her.

In the back of her mind, Quita wanted to tell the doctor she didn't need sympathy. But the words wouldn't come, and the saddest part of her accepted the doctor's graciousness. "There's fallopian tube damage. Could have been a terrible fall or a car accident. Who knows?"

"A car accident." Quita tried to pull herself together. "But that was so long ago. Twenty-two years ago."

The doctor nodded. "Were you wearing a seat belt?"

"Yes."

"Without knowing any of the history, I can tell by the ultrasound that you sustained damage to your lower abdomen. Scar tissue formed and over the years began to block the tubes. One tube is fully closed. The other is more than eighty percent blocked."

Helpless anger rose. "They said I was okay. They sent us home. I was sore, but after a few weeks, the pain went away."

"I can't defend the doctors. They missed it. There was damage."

Quita had always heard that the thing you wanted most was the most difficult to obtain. This was proof. "Surgery?" she asked. "Is that a possibility?"

"For the fibroids, yes. Damage to the fallopian tubes is irreversible."

Her last hope died. Air filled her ears. Quita closed her eyes and tried to see the baby she dreamed about. But no images of the chubby boy with curly locks and a happy smile came to mind.

She wasn't ever going to be a mother. "I'd better go." Quita stood up and accepted the tissue from Dr. Tate. She needed to be out of there and someplace where she could rage and get this out of her system.

"We're not done." The woman's strong Irish features were stubbornly set.

Quita sat down.

"I know you want to go home and curl into a ball—"

"Please don't tell me you've been here. Platitudes are wasted on me."

"Good, because I've never been good at giving them. There are possibilities, and since the clock is ticking, we should make some decisions today."

Quita shied away from hoping. "I'm listening."

"Have you ever thought about adoption?"

"I want my own child for personal reasons." How could she explain that she wanted to look into the eyes of her own child and convey the depths of her love from her touch to his, her eyes to his, her heart to his? Her child, born of her body, would know of his mother's love. She didn't think she could love another woman's child that way. "I don't want to adopt a child. I'm willing to take on the full responsibility of single parenthood for my baby and me. Nothing else is an option."

"What about marriage? Have you thought about it? Marriage might be enough," Tate suggested.

"I haven't met a man willing to be in my life my way. I sacrificed too much growing up. I want a child. A husband isn't an absolute requirement."

Doctor Tate reached for her chewed-up Bic pen and a card.

"I'd like you to see Dr. Amir Buzu. He's a fertility specialist that I personally worked with ten years ago. He's at Emory."

"You? Personally?"

"Yes."

"What was wrong, if you don't mind my asking?"

Ann's mouth turned into a half smile. "I needed help getting pregnant. He helped me."

"Was he successful?" she said quietly.

Doctor Tate pulled pictures from the shelf behind her. "Two boys and a girl."

Quita stared hungrily at the photos. "Triplets? Wow. They're beautiful, but I just want one little boy."

"I'm not sure Dr. Buzu can be that specific, but for me it was a one-shot deal. I'm sure you've heard of in vitro fertilization."

"Yes, but I don't know much about it." Reeling, Quita focused on the ray of hope the doctor cast her way.

" 'In vitro' means to extract a viable egg from the mother, fertilize it outside the woman's body with a man's sperm, and insert the fertilized egg into the womb. The benefit is that if your uterus is healthy, you can carry the baby to term like anyone else."

"But you said my uterus—" Quita stumbled. "I have fibroid tumors."

"Correct, but if you choose in vitro fertilization, I'd wait for a second opinion."

"Okay, but what's the downside?"

"You have to follow a regimen of vitamins and shots, and you might conceive and then miscarry. This could happen multiple times before you have a baby. The emotional roller coaster can be difficult. Cost is among the most major factors, besides the body rejecting the fertilization."

"I have insurance."

Doctor Tate's posture grew less rigid. "This procedure isn't covered by your health insurance. It can get fairly expensive."

Anxiety tightened Quita's chest and she allowed the arrows of truth to sting her guilty conscience. She had made and blown so much money over the past ten years, but had very little saved up for a rainy day. Now she was in the midst of hurricane season, and she was drowning. "How much?"

"Seven to ten thousand per session."

Quita's mouth dried. Her bank balance would only cover one attempt. "How many times does it usually take?"

"There are no guarantees."

"Ann—" Quita broke in, tired of the obligatory caveats to the truth. "Give it to me in realistic numbers. What is the average?"

"Okay, Marquita, three to four or more."

Her breath whooshed out and seconds later she heard Dr. Tate say, "Breathe. In and out slowly. Marquita, can you hear me?"

Quita inhaled against the burning in her chest. The doctor eased a cup of water to her lips, murmuring soothing words. "Nothing has to be decided today."

They were quiet for a long time. "I don't have much time."

"Sure you do. You're young."

She couldn't tell the doctor that after a certain point, she would walk away with her garbage bag of hurt on her shoulder and not look back.

Unknown quantities hurt the most, and up until now, she'd been damn good at avoiding them. But this bitch of pain threatened to eat her alive. How ironic that it hurt worse than finding out she didn't have a daddy who cared and loved her. This was worse than her boyfriend choosing her sister over her, and it hurt worse than being put out of her mother's house for kicking her sister and her *ex*-man's ass.

Nothing hurt worse than this.

All she wanted was one little baby.

God must not want her to have a child.

Determination made her fight, not in defiance to the Lord, but in deference to herself. "What do I need to do?"

"We'll set up your appointment with Doctor Buzu. He'll complete psychological and physical testing. If he determines you're not ready, he won't proceed."

This time when Quita got up, stubborn grit kept her erect.

"I'm going to do whatever it takes to get that money, and I can take whatever he throws at me."

Tate didn't look away as the silence stretched. "I'm glad for you."

Quita bit her trembling lower lip. "Thank you."

In the car, Quita wouldn't let herself cry.

There were always stories about people who'd been diagnosed with something, and the doctors ended up being wrong.

She hit the gas pedal on I-285 West, leaving the Perimeter behind, and made up her mind. She'd go see Dr. Buzu, but she'd keep on trying to get pregnant the old-fashioned way. She dialed Jimmy and left a message. If anybody could get her pregnant, it was the ever-ready Jimmy.

But as she drove home, the thought snuck in.

If she couldn't have a baby, what was the purpose of her life?

Chapter 8
BJ

"BJ, you know I want you. Let me come in."

With her back pressed into the molding around her front door, BJ had to admit it felt good to have a man against her.

Mike made her feel short and feminine. He knew just how to push her buttons.

But Mike was the type of man she'd always avoided.

Musicians and professional athletes weren't so different. Fidelity was optional, and she wanted someone who wanted only her.

But Big Squirt felt good.

A shiver curled through her as he did things with his tongue against her breasts.

Ride the wave, she thought, but not in her front yard.

Caution overrode lust and forced her knees toward each other. Mike groaned when the vice grip from her thighs disrupted his rhythmic grind. "Baby, let's go inside."

"I don't know—"

She saw intelligence and passion as his gaze searched hers for a shimmer of permission, and when they met indecision, they slanted like the neck of a cobra and began the "please, baby, baby, please" dance.

This kind of flattery had gotten him from first base earlier, to a near home run now.

She unlocked the door, and he reached around her and pushed it open.

He hooked his fingers inside the waistband of her Anne Klein slacks and tugged her toward the stairs. "Now, BJ."

Things were moving at warp speed. She stumbled on the second step, and he broke her tumble with one arm and followed her down. BJ felt as light as air.

Maybe this was right.

Maybe there weren't any "rules" except the ones she'd imposed upon herself.

Bleep. Bleep. Bleep.

She stayed in the moment and raised her hand to his cheek, seeking greater depth to their kiss.

Bleep. Bleep. Bleep.

Mike kept his mouth on hers, but pulled his beeper from his hip and tried to read the screen from the corner of his eye.

No he didn't.

Her combat-boots-wearing conscience kicked her into reality. BJ shoved. "It's time for you to go." The sex-starved woman in her railed. After all, she was the one with her blouse open, her heart on top of her bra. But the fire in his eyes had died.

Damnit. She was just another lay.

"Let me stay," he said simply. He didn't even have it in him to beg.

She shook her head.

Just like that, he walked out and left the door open.

BJ sat on the stairs, listening to him drive away, and she squeezed her eyes shut. "What the hell was I thinking?"

She rested her chin on her hand. She'd remember this night ten years from now and still be embarrassed.

She thanked God her grandmother no longer lived with her. One guilty conscience was enough.

Her chest started to sting and BJ looked down and smashed a mosquito that found her breast more appetizing than Mike had.

The bite bloomed. "That's what I get."

Getting up, she yanked her shirt closed and shut the door. Why had she brought that fool home?

Yesterday he'd wanted to come by, cook for her and the girls, and today at lunch sexual tension should have been an appetizer on the menu.

She'd made the mistake of offering him her evening, but he wouldn't commit, so she'd ended up at Café 290, with an attitude and a desire to show herself that she could pull any man she wanted.

Mike had walked into the club, talked big game, and here she'd landed. With a big bite on her tittie and her pride smashed against her palm.

BJ kicked off her shoes, walked toward the court, and flipped on the outdoor lights. She dragged out the ball rack and laced on her sneakers. The pimpled rubber of her basketball grazed her hand, and she caressed it before letting it fall and bounce back.

It felt good. Basketball was something she understood.

She dropped the ball again, wanting to expunge Mike from her mind. But each time the wind blew against a place where his mouth or hands had been, she thought of *his hands gliding across her skin.*

She bounced the ball again and started trotting.

His mouth on her neck.

She tried to jog away from her thoughts.

His leg between hers.

She jumped.

Her foot on her own ass for being stupid.

She slammed the ball home.

BJ landed on the court, laughing.

The guilt fell away with the perspiration. She put the ball away, and was pulling the rack when the phone rang. She snatched up her cell. "Hello?"

"Hey."

"Quita?" BJ slapped her forehead. She'd forgotten all about her doctor's appointment. "Hey, how did things go?"

"I have *bad* bad news and bad news."

BJ's stomach flopped as she dried herself with a hand towel. "What's the *bad* bad news?"

"I can't make babies the regular way." Quita's voice was barely audible.

BJ slipped onto a breakfast stool. "What? What does that mean? I mean, I know what it means, but why not?"

"My fallopian tubes are blocked. One completely and the other eighty percent or something."

Silence hung between them as BJ searched for the right words. None came.

"Don't you dare say you're sorry," Quita bossed. "That's one thing I love about you, BJ. You never go for those fake crap sayings that people use just to make themselves feel better. You know I hate that. Don't you dare—" she said, and broke off on a sob.

BJ leaned against the counter, her hand over her eyes. "What can I do?"

Quita's watery sigh floated through the phone lines. "You got forty thousand dollars?"

"What?" BJ exhaled in disbelief.

"That's what in vitro fertilization costs."

BJ's legs collapsed and she crossed them. "Whoa, okay? First we're talking about your fallopian tubes being blocked, and now we're talking about a forty-thousand dollar in vitro fertilization. I didn't even know you were trying to have a baby."

"Well, now you know."

"Why?" BJ demanded. "You're not married—and you don't have

to be, but I always thought you'd do one before the other. I'm going in circles, but—" She stopped. "I don't know what to say."

"Why do I need a husband? Mama, Aunt Lou, Gloria, my cousins—none of them have men and they're fine."

But you're different from them, BJ wanted to say, but didn't.

"You don't need one, Quita. I just thought . . ."

"Yeah, me, too. You got forty grand?"

BJ couldn't touch her retirement for anything. "No, Sweetie. I wish I did."

Quita's chuckle filled with tears. "Join the club."

How could they be two successful women with all of the accoutrements of success, but no money?

"What are you thinking?" Quita asked.

"That we're pathetic."

Quita laughed and BJ joined her. "True that." The intensity lessened.

"How long have you been trying?"

"A while," Quita's voice grew smaller.

BJ tried to keep the shock inside. Quita didn't need her to stand in judgment. But that explained a lot. "That's why the steady train of men?"

Quita sighed. "Yeah. I guess I always knew something wasn't right."

"You've been playing roulette, Quita. You have to know you're worth more than that."

"I want a baby, BJ, and that means more to me than anything in the world."

In a weird way, BJ understood. "I'm coming over."

"Don't. I'm fine."

Pushing herself up, BJ shut off the outdoor lights and pulled on a button-up shirt from the laundry room. "Look, I've got a friend over there who needs a hug. If she ain't you, then step aside. Besides, I've got a hickey on my tit, and my friend will want to know how it got there."

Quita sucked in a surprised breath. "What the hell you been up to, Tramp?"

BJ locked the front door and got into her car. "No, you didn't," she said with mock indignation. "One of us needs to go to church next Sunday, and I think that would be you."

Quita was quiet for a moment. "I think you're right."

This was a night for surprises. BJ took her hand off the keyed ignition. "I'm going to pick up Ebony, and we'll be there in thirty minutes, okay?"

She took a chance, given Ebony and Quita's friction lately. But they were great friends and Ebony was the most religious of the group. Right now, they needed someone who could pray.

"Okay," Quita finally said. "Hurry."

Chapter 9
Ebony

"Ebony! Why you got the door locked? I been callin' you for ten minutes!"

Ruby Dee's voice startled Ebony, and she dropped the eye shadow brush. Passion pink dust splattered across the towel she'd used to protect the comforter, before she could put it back into the tray. This makeup stuff was difficult.

As she unlocked her bedroom door, she tried to wipe the makeup from her eye. "What is it, Mama?"

"That girl keeps calling. I told her it was too late to be ringing somebody, but yo' friends ain't got no respect."

"What girl?"

"One of them two that always call. It ain't like you got a long list."

"Was it BJ?" Ebony tried to ignore her mother's insults. The woman was so negative, she'd find the bad in a baby christening.

"I said I don't know."

"Did she curse you out?"

"Ain't nobody cursing me out."

"Then it was BJ."

"That other one is just evil. If she was my daughter, I'd have taken my cane to her long ago."

How many times had Ebony heard that? Ruby Dee Manchester was sixty, bitter, and damn near crippled, but she hadn't always been that way. Once upon a time, Ruby Dee had been a beauty queen, a winner in the Miss Black Teen Georgia. She'd gone on to qualify in the Miss Black America contest, but Ulysses Manchester had been too much of a lure. She'd married, and her life changed drastically. She'd become a postman's wife. Trapped in a life she couldn't stand, with a husband and daughter she blamed for derailing her career.

When Ulysses died, she merely heaped that blame onto her daughter's shoulders. Up until last year, Ebony had tried to please her; now she tried hard not to hate her mother.

Ruby Dee got real close and squinted in Ebony's face. "What the hell you doin' in here? You look like a schizophrenic got a hold of you."

"Get out," Ebony said firmly. Before her mother had moved in with her, Ebony remembered liking herself. In rare moments, she'd even liked her mother. Now, nothing Ebony ever did was right, and sometimes she believed the vile words that spewed from Ruby Dee's mouth. "Now, Mama."

"I'm just saying, that stuff ain't gone help you none. You took after your daddy there."

"Mama, I'm busy. I don't have time for this right now." Ebony slammed the door and covered her eyes. "Jesus, Jesus, Jesus," she said to the ceiling. "Deliver me!"

"I'm old and frail," her mother moaned, going down the stairs. "I took good care of you. And it's your turn to take care of me. You hear that?" she shrieked, before starting to hum the hymn with no name that Ebony had entitled "Long Suffering."

Anytime Ruby Dee didn't get her way, she'd start humming and shuffling.

Two years was a long time to heal from knee-replacement

surgery, but her mother blamed the doctor and not herself for her continued health problems. The truth was, she was lazy and fat.

When she'd applied for worker's compensation from her job on the assembly line at the mattress factory, they'd approved her in record time. Ebony had never been aware of any work-related injury, but they'd found a way to not take her back.

Ruby Dee was supposed to have moved in with Ebony for a few weeks while her knee healed, and then gone back to her rent-subsidized apartment. That day had never come.

Then sixteen months ago, Aunt Jo came for a visit and never left.

Ebony was stuck with two old women who swore they had somewhere else to go, but didn't seem in a hurry to get there.

She turned up the stereo in her overcrowded room and went back to her bed. Everything that she'd purchased for her new house had been crammed into this room when they'd moved in.

This rental property was supposed to have been temporary housing until she found the perfect three-bedroom, two-and-a-half-bathroom ranch house.

Every day Ebony dreamed about her house and she knew that homeownership would come soon. She couldn't take them much longer.

In the lighted mirror, she saw how she'd extended eye shadow to her temple, and had gotten some on her nose, and how the top color didn't look at all like the picture the lady at the makeup counter had given her when she'd made her two-hundred-dollar purchase.

Ebony's hopes deflated. Here she was trying to save every dime to buy a house, and she'd just spent good money on makeup that made her look crazy.

She suppressed the thought that her mother might be right. Grabbing the towel, she scrubbed her face in frustration that she wasn't naturally pretty, naturally graceful, naturally anything—except plain.

A knock on her door brought her head up sharply. "What is it?"

BJ stuck her head inside. "Hey. Your mother is down there screaming, you're up here screaming, no wonder everybody in this house has high blood pressure. Come on before somebody in here has a stroke."

Relief socked Ebony in the chest. "Can I spend the night?"

BJ's eyes grew wide. "Only if Cruella and her twin don't have my home phone number."

"They don't."

Ebony grabbed all of her stuff, locked her room door, and sprinted out of the house, ignoring her mother's shout for milk from the store. They could damn well get their own milk.

"What's the matter?" she asked BJ, who hadn't commented on her makeup or the reason for visiting at eleven o'clock at night.

"Quita got some bad news." BJ took a big breath. "She can't have children."

"Oh my God." Ebony didn't know what to say.

BJ nodded. "She's taking it pretty hard."

Why hadn't Quita called her? "When did she find out?"

"Sometime today. I just talked to her a little while ago."

They eventually got on 285 West and exited at Covington Road, her tires squealing. "We want to get there in one piece, please."

"Sorry," BJ apologized. "Did you know she's been wanting a baby for a while?"

"I had no idea." The news *was* shocking. But Quita had surprised her a lot lately. When she'd taken up for Ebony in the club and then proclaimed that they were best friends, Ebony had been stunned. But by her rules, best friends shared everything. Even bad news. Why hadn't Quita called her before BJ?

A tinge of anger pulsed through her at the idea that BJ was so concerned about Quita. When Ebony'd had gallstones last year, had either of them come running to her in the middle of the night? No. She'd toughed it out alone at Piedmont Hospital, and by the time they'd visited, she'd been home for two days.

So Quita couldn't have babies. There were tons of kids without homes. Why not adopt one of them? Besides, she had the rest of the world in the palm of her hand. "She's got the restaurant and club, a house, and she's gorgeous," Ebony said, exasperated. "I don't know why she'd want to give up her freedom for kids."

"That's so judgmental."

"It's just us talking, BJ. Nobody's here but you, me, and the trees. All I'm saying is that she's got a picture-perfect life. You see the hell I go through every day. Frankly, if I never have children, that's fine with me."

BJ's hands rose and fell off the steering wheel. Lights from cars on 285 winked as they crossed over the interstate.

"You feel that way because your mother and aunt are—no offense—terrible people who take advantage of you."

They parked outside of Quita's house. Nothing moved in the exclusive neighborhood, except the extinguishing lights of residents turning in.

The peace and quiet Ebony craved rolled from the lush bushes into her body and rocked her soul. She wanted this more than anything.

"I don't know a woman alive who doesn't want to have kids," BJ said.

Ebony eyed her curiously. "Nobody?"

"You would be the first."

The last thing she wanted was to be ostracized by her only friends. "I'm not trying to make light of her pain. I don't want you to think that way about me."

"You're entitled to your opinion."

Ebony scrambled. "That's not my opinion, you misunderstood me. I don't want you to tell Quita—"

"I wouldn't tell her anything. I'm scared, Ebony. She was crying."

"Wow."

"What are we going to say?" BJ wanted to know.

Ebony opened the door and got out. "I'll take my cues from her. That's what best friends do."

She felt BJ's gaze on her as she walked up the dark path to the front door.

At the right time, Ebony'd mention to Quita about calling her when she needed a friend. After all, that's what best friends were for.

Chapter 10
Quita

Every pot on the stove bubbled to sufficient levels as Quita forced her thoughts to recipes she'd learned at Mimi's knee. She needed to reach out to her spirit today in the hopes that Mimi could comfort her as she had when she'd been alive.

As she sipped Hennessey and apple juice from a twelve-ounce glass, she eyed BJ and Ebony. "Stop looking at me, damnit, I'm fine."

They'd never seen her cry, and from their stricken expressions, they didn't want to see it again. Quita wiped her eyes on her crying dish towel and pulled a bucket of fresh lobster out of the refrigerator.

"That's right, you're going to taste delicious. Get in there," she said as she dropped the crustaceans into boiling water. "Do you know what gets me?" Quita secured the lid on the pot and propped her back against the tile counter. "I had to convince Buzu I was worthy of a child. I'm a respectable, responsible, successful woman, and I have to justify wanting a kid. Addicts make them for free! Something is definitely wrong with the system. It's not fair." Her eyes brimmed again.

This time BJ came around the island. "Why don't you slow down a minute, and tell us everything the doctor said."

Quita looked inside her glass for answers.

"Should you be drinking that?" Ebony murmured.

Quita lifted the glass in a toast. "Yes, damnit, because I'm no more pregnant than those delicious lobsters are alive. By the way, they should be done. All we need is asparagus and melted butter, and we're ready to feast."

"I'm not really hungry, Quita." BJ trailed her. "I'm worried about you."

Quita couldn't stop her heart from squeezing. "I'm glad," she said, and sighed over her glass. "Everybody thinks I'm tough, and I am, aren't I? Don't I inspire fear?"

Ebony nodded like a bobble-head doll. "Yes, you do. What did the doctor say?"

"She recommended I see a specialist. I have fibroids and endometriosis. Apparently, I've been walking around with this since I was eight years old. Isn't that irony for you? Some people become lawyers, some people become mothers. I am Quita. I have endometriosis," she announced. "That's it. The sum total of who and what I am."

"No," they disagreed together.

"You're right, it's who I am tonight." She dished up the lobster, vegetables, butter, and drinks all the way around.

She walked into the dining room with her plate and a glass, and BJ and Ebony stayed in the kitchen. "If you don't come eat with me, you won't know what I've decided to do." Quita knew she was pushing BJ's patience, but she could only deal with *her* emotions right now.

BJ stuck her head around the corner. "I'll join you if you stop drinking."

Quita had the glass halfway to her mouth. "After this one, okay?"

"The very last."

Four slugs and a healthy burp later, the three of them slipped on their bibs and got down to business.

"When's your appointment?" BJ asked.

Quita closed her eyes. "Next week."

"Why are you trying to get pregnant? You have a great life as far as I'm concerned," Ebony told her matter-of-factly.

"Is that what you think, too?" Quita turned to BJ, who despite her protest ate just as much as they did.

"I've met your family and I don't know why you'd ever want to go there."

"Amen," Ebony added, "but I'm speaking from my own perspective. I'm convinced my mother had me just to have something over my dad's head. Lucky for him, he died young."

"Well, damn." Quita didn't see her mother and aunts all that much, and yes, they were dysfunctional, but they were still her people. But BJ had met them before and seen firsthand the level of their distrust of men. "Eb," Quita said, "I guess we're too screwed up to procreate with our busted-up family history."

"BJ, too," Ebony added.

Even buzzed, Quita could see that BJ didn't like her comment.

"I *never* knew my mother, and I don't know *what* her problems were, so don't drag her into your pity fest. I'm trying to figure out why a successful woman like you wants to have a baby by herself."

BJ's uncharacteristic defense of her mother rubbed on Quita's nerves. "Why would you wonder that? Why aren't you searching for answers to the riddles in your life?"

BJ's bib hit the table. "I didn't come here to defend myself. I thought you needed moral support. If you're fine, I'm going home. I have a job to get up for in the morning."

"It may sound stupid to you," Quita said, hoping she wouldn't leave, "but I want a baby to love."

BJ kneeled down and clutched Quita's hand. "I've always supported you. The restaurant, the investment club, and even this silly date-night thing. You know I've got your back. But you're talking about raising a kid alone and it's hard. My grandmother and I struggled through some really tough times. If it weren't for me being able to play ball, I don't know what would have happened to us."

"I know."

Murky memories clouded BJ's eyes and she looked like a lost child. Quita had been raised by her own mother, but didn't feel she'd turned out any better than either of her two friends. But Quita knew herself better than BJ and Ebony gave her credit for. "I have a great job. I'm healthy except in that one area. If I have a baby, we'll be all right."

"Wouldn't 'right' be with the father of the baby?" Ebony pointed out, looking between the two of them with a bewildered expression on her face.

"Do you see a man around here?" Quita demanded. "Have you seen me with anyone that you'd consider good husband material? Why should I put my dreams on hold for that special someone who may not exist? No! Accept my decision or get off my merry-go-round. My mind is made up."

"Can I say something before you run off with your Gucci backpack and claim you don't have any friends?" BJ said as she sat down.

Quita couldn't keep the smile from her aching cheeks. "What?"

"Visit your cousin Ivy and see what it's going to be like. Get first-hand experience on the life of a single mother. That's all I ask."

Quita's first instinct was to say no, but BJ, in her infinite wisdom, had a point. Ivy was the one relative who, like Quita, didn't buy into the "I hate men" theory until the man actually messed up. "Okay, but only if you tell me how you got that goose on your tittie."

Ebony's crabcracker clattered to the table and her head whipped around. "When did that happen?"

BJ's cheeks flamed. "This little soiree isn't about me, and it's late." She tried to adjust her blouse, but Quita snagged back the lapel. "You promised. Oooh. He got you good. Was it Mike?"

At first, BJ looked like she didn't want to say. "Yeah."

"Who's he?" Ebony demanded.

"The musician from Taboo." She didn't smile. Quita's drunken state didn't stop her heart from aching for her friend.

"I didn't know you were seeing him," Ebony said, as if they'd intentionally kept the info from her.

"I'm not." The flush on BJ's cheeks crept higher. "Nothing happened. His beeper went off, and after the second time, I told him to go."

"Good." Quita tried to control her slurring voice and gave up. "Don't let him get away with sh-shit. Course if he can make magic between the sheets, keep him until you feel real good, then send him home. Damn, I need another drink." She grabbed Ebony's untouched glass and swallowed. The potency didn't dull the pain enough. She could still feel it in her chest like a bad case of indigestion. Her neck was heavy and her ears warm. She didn't want to cry anymore. Crying reminded her that there was pain.

They sat around the once gleaming dining room table, filled with the ravages of her anger.

"What will you do if this second-opinion doctor agrees with the first?"

"You know, Ebony, what can I do? I choose to look at the positive. I'll get the second, then I'll decide my next move." Quita sighed. "Anybody want some cobbler? Mimi's cobbler is delicious."

BJ picked at her asparagus. "I can't mix liquor and dessert. Want me to stay over?"

Quita wanted her to, but didn't. "No. Go home and get some rest."

"I don't have to leave right now."

"I'll stay with her," Ebony offered, her arms crossed, a navy doo rag around her head.

"You look like a black tin soldier." Quita burst out laughing and BJ joined her.

Ebony's smile was tremulous. "Laugh away. I'm going to start cleaning the kitchen." She started humming and Quita wanted to ask if that was the long-suffering song Ebony's mother often sang. It didn't have a particular rhythm, or a distinct melody, but it made her want to holler.

"Shhhhh," she said, her lips flapping. "No singing." Her head fell forward. "Go home, Ebony. You're stressing me out."

"Go to sleep and the stress will go away." Ebony started removing dishes from the table, adding a soprano clang to the buzz saw that vibrated from Quita's head to her tailbone.

BJ followed her into the kitchen. "Ebony, let's go. We can clean up tomorrow. Let's just get her into bed."

"I don't mind." Their voices grew faint. "What do you think she'll do if she doesn't have a baby?" Ebony couldn't whisper for anything.

"As much as she wants a baby, I don't know. I just hope she doesn't have any more nights like this."

"Sometimes, people don't need much to go over the edge," Ebony said morbidly.

Chills raced over Quita.

"You'd better not ever let me hear you say that again. Good grief, Ebony." BJ threw silverware into the sink. "I'm putting her to bed. You clean up."

How could Ebony know that Quita felt as if she were looking over the edge now?

Chapter 11
BJ

Outside the Georgia Pacific building, BJ could feel the heat penetrate her sandals and cook the soles of her feet.

The brutal sun had played hopscotch with Mother Nature and brought summer nearly two months early. And there was no end in sight.

She wished someone could burn last night from her brain, but Quita's sad, drunken state had left indelible tracks on BJ's psyche until she'd had to consciously put the situation out of her mind. Otherwise, she couldn't think about anything else.

Even through it all, BJ admired Quita. Her honesty tore the pretense off BJ's cartoonish existence. Last night she'd dreamed about her own life with a child. Although she hadn't been able to see a face, she'd heard the crying and had felt her heartstrings tugged. In the brutal light of day she knew she wasn't ready for a baby, but a grown man to love, that was a different story.

BJ tried not to inhale the heat too deeply, to allow her lungs time to adjust as she walked. The Underground wasn't far, and she wanted time out of the building of processed air and fluorescent lighting.

Ahead, bums congregated on the sidewalk, swaying and jerking, as if harassing her took special energy. These men were her age in years, but a hundred more in life.

"Hey, baby, you sho is cute. Can a brotha get five dollars?"

"No." She walked faster, but a bold one fell in step a couple paces behind her.

"What you got against helping a brotha out?"

"You have legs," she said, and increased her stride before she turned the corner.

"So what? I got legs? I need money."

"If you have legs, you can work." A man on a makeshift board with wheels, no legs, and a cup tied around his neck moved forward when he saw her. She dropped two dollars in his cup and kept moving.

Her adversary followed her. "So that's all there is? You help one man and not me? You don't know nothin' about me, but you assume I'm beggin' because I don't want to work."

BJ wished now that she'd driven her car to her meeting at Mick's at the Underground. The hassle she was going through wasn't worth it.

She turned around, aggravated. "You're intelligent enough to argue your point, but not enough to show up for a job? I don't owe you anything."

"I guess black don't help black no more."

BJ had reached the Underground and turned to see the man talking into his shabby coat. He might have needed help, but he'd pissed her off.

All her life she'd had to struggle for everything. But there'd been a time long ago when she'd needed help. And she'd had two legs. She gave him two dollars. "Here. Now get a damned job."

She turned to go inside and felt a hard yank on her purse before a searing pain shot through her arm. The pain didn't stop her from fighting back. Off balance, she fell to her knees half in, half out of the building. Screaming resonated around her and someone landed on her. Her head smacked the floor hard.

"Stop fighting! We got him. Stop!" A man pressed forcefully into her chest. Air burst from her lungs, leaving her weak and seeing stars.

"Take it easy," he shouted at her. "We recovered your purse."

BJ struggled to focus. The bum was on top of her!

She grabbed his hand and twisted, but froze when she saw his badge.

"I'm a cop."

He was on his knees, and he looked scared of the impending pain.

She was just scared. BJ lay back on the floor. "What the hell . . . ? What happened to me?"

She tried to sit up but her hands shook. She planted them firmly on the floor, forced her elbows straight, and breathed deeply. There were people everywhere, uniformed cops who surrounded the suspect and then led him away. He was the man from the board, who, strangely enough, had legs.

BJ fought to get up and grimaced. The bum/cop put his dirty hands on her shoulder. "Lay down."

She flinched and felt like crying. "The floor is dirty."

"We need a paramedic," he called to about a dozen Underground security officers.

"I'm okay." Her arms quivered and she gave up. She wasn't okay.

His hands tunneled through her hair and she shook him free and was rewarded with firecrackers blasting behind her eyelids. "Ow."

"Told you to stay down."

"What just happened?"

"You were mugged. Be still and we'll have you taken care of in no time. You won't panic, right?"

"No. What's your name?" BJ managed to say without tears, surprised at herself. She'd been in tougher street fights and hadn't cried. If she kept talking she'd calm down. She looked at him through her fingers.

"Keiko Riggs, undercover officer, Atlanta PD. Yours?" he asked.

"BJ."

He shook his head. "You are one Beverly Jason, and you played for the Washington Flames. Had a helluva outside jumper—when you were mad. Competitive on the court. Retired two years ago."

How would he know that? Had he been spying on her? Was this some kind of spy-cam crap?

"How do you know who I am?"

"Last year my daughter had to do a paper on a local sports figure. She chose you."

Words didn't come right away. Here was a man who wasn't as he appeared, who knew things about her she hadn't expected. She'd been turned off by his filthiness although he'd just rescued her. BJ tried to roll to her side. "I think I can sit up now."

His hand landed on her shoulder again. "You smacked your head pretty hard. You have a knot on the back of your head."

She was hurt. BJ couldn't believe it.

"You should have let him have your purse."

"Why? It's mine."

"Think of it this way; sometimes it's better to give up something to maintain what you've got."

This time when she looked at him, there were no stars. "What's that supposed to mean?"

"Had you not been arguing with me, you'd have noticed the man following you, and you'd have protected yourself. Good, the cavalry is here."

BJ wanted to tell him he started the fight, that if he hadn't been harassing her, she'd have noticed the other man, but she didn't have time. The paramedic's arrival created pandemonium. BJ felt as if she were on the basketball court again.

Once, she'd been shoved into the goalpost and had been unconscious for a couple seconds. The entire stadium had watched. When she'd gotten up, they'd given her a standing ovation.

That better not happen today. Keiko Riggs kneeled beside her while speaking to the paramedic. "She's aware and lucid. She's got a knot on the back of her head, and she's asked to sit up twice."

The paramedics moved him aside and took over. BJ answered questions, let them give her an exam, and they helped her to a sitting position. Her blouse had been torn in the struggle and she clutched the yellow silk. Thankfully, her jacket was only dirty and she buttoned it to cover her skin.

"I'm okay," she told them. "I just want to get back to work."

"We should really take you to Grady and have you checked out."

"I'm not going to the hospital. If I feel worse later, I'll call my primary care physician. Really, I'm good. Help me up, please?"

It took both paramedics to hoist her up and for a moment she almost wished she'd stayed on the ground, but after a few seconds of flexing and trying out her legs, she was steadier. Thankfully, there was no clapping.

"Feeling better, Ms. Jason?"

"Yes. Thank you. I just need my shoes and maybe a ride back to work." She scribbled her name on the release form.

An officer from the Underground gave her one shoe. "We couldn't find the other one."

"Where's Officer Riggs? He might know."

"He went back to the station with the suspect," a uniformed cop told her.

"Did he have my shoe when he left?"

"I didn't see him with any evidence bags."

BJ took the one shoe. "No purse either?" She sighed and wiped her burning eyes. "What station does he work at?"

"Fourteen. Ma'am, we're giving you a ride. This way, please."

Her arm was sore and a headache percolated at the base of her head. BJ trailed one officer while the other pulled up the rear. "Can you get a message to Officer Riggs and tell him I said to call me?"

"Sure," he said, as if she'd have a better chance of frying an egg on the sidewalk.

The door was held for her and BJ was thrust back into the bright sunshine. The ground was unmerciful and she was glad to slip into the back of the cruiser. Two minutes later she was back in her building. Word had gotten out and her boss greeted her in the lobby. "Take the rest of the day off and get yourself looked at."

"I'm fine."

"Yeah, I heard that from Officer Riggs, but I want to hear it from a medical professional."

Startled, BJ looked up at Robin Jacobi. "You know him?"

"I met him yesterday when he stopped by the office and told me to stop calling the cops on him. Apparently, he's doing surveillance against petty criminals who prey on unsuspecting victims."

Angry, she hobbled toward the elevator. "No one thought to tell the women in the building that we're sitting ducks?"

Robin wasn't bothered by her shortness. He guided her into the elevator and pushed twelve.

"No."

Her mouth fell open.

"BJ," he said, cutting her off. "Women talk. Next thing you know, the whole building knows, and what happens when they take it out on the homeless men? The men become more aggressive and then someone really does get hurt. The police were handling it."

He was right. What could she say? Her own moral code had proven skewed, but she didn't feel like beating herself up. The thief had taken care of that for her. She glanced at her watch. "I was on my way to a meeting with the reps from Nike. I have to get over there."

He waved down her sudden panic. "Stop worrying. I'll take care of it. You're going home."

They exited on twelve and her assistant was waiting. "No shoes?"

BJ showed her the one in her hand. "That's it. Robin insists I go home. Anything pressing to stop me?"

"Where's your purse?"

"I don't know." Frustrated, BJ headed toward her office, her hip aching.

"Getting sore?" Robin encouraged her to use his extended arm.

"Yeah, a little."

"You're almost thirty-one," he said, with a smile on his fifty-year-old face. "Tomorrow you'll be black and blue. Happens when you get old."

Despite herself, she giggled as he helped her into her office chair. He and Teresa stared at her, worried. "Can I get some clean clothes and sneakers from Hawks Place?" she asked, referring to their in-house store for players and staff.

"Yes, of course." Robin used her phone and ordered an outfit she pointed to from the summer line. "Teresa, would you mind going to get those items? I'll stay until you get back. Then this lady needs to get home."

BJ appreciated her boss's protectiveness—he had four adopted daughters—but she didn't need a babysitter. "Robin, go take care of our clients. I promise not to leave this chair until Teresa comes back."

"Okay." He looked worried. Like a good father would. BJ felt a pang of sorrow. She'd never known this type of caring. From any man.

"Go ahead, sir. I'll be fine."

"Will you call when you get home? How will you get in your house if your purse is gone? Do you have a spare key?"

Now he was making her worry.

"I've got a way to get in."

He stared at her blankly. "Of course a friend will let you in. Call me here once you get there, okay?"

BJ smiled. "Promise." She didn't lean her head back until the door to her office closed. Then she closed her eyes. What a day.

Her stomach growled. That's why she'd been so happy to go to the Underground. She loved Mick's.

There's gum in my purse.

BJ dialed directory assistance. "Atlanta. The number for police station fourteen, please."

The number was given automatically, but she wrote it down then pressed one. "Officer Keiko Riggs, please."

"Just a moment."

While she waited, BJ wasn't sure what she was going to say. "Detective Riggs."

"You didn't tell me you were a detective."

"Who is this?"

"Beverly Jason," she said, angry that she could be so easily forgotten.

"Hello, Beverly. How are you feeling?"

"Ripped off."

He laughed. "And why is that?"

"Because I'm minus a purse."

"Ah."

She waited for more but none came. "Well?"

"Well, what?"

"Why'd you leave with my bag?"

"Because then I'd have another reason to talk to you. And, I had to log the evidence."

"How am I supposed to get home?"

"You don't have a spare set of keys?"

"You stole my purse, and my shoe."

"I'm pleading not guilty to that."

"When can I get my stuff back?"

Teresa entered with the new clothes and BJ put him on speaker while she changed.

"When do you want them?"

"Now would be good so I can go home."

"I'll drive you," Teresa offered.

BJ waved at Teresa to shut up. "Thanks, I have a car. If *someone* brought my purse back, I could drive myself home."

"You don't need to be driving. Besides, that knot felt significant."

"Don't tell me what to do. Teresa, aspirin, please?"

"If you go to the doctor, I'll bring them by later," Riggs said.

Teresa's eyebrows shot up and BJ tugged on the sleeveless skin-tight tank top. "You thought this was a good idea?" she said to Teresa.

"Sorry," they both replied.

"Riggs, I'm not talking to you. Skin tight *and* pink, Teresa? Nothing in red or white?"

"Sorry, boss." Teresa gave her the water and pain pills. "I'm going to finish up some stuff at my desk. Just come out when you're ready to go."

BJ's head pounded as she finished lacing up the sneakers. "Riggs, I want my property tonight."

"Okay, where do you live?"

"You're a cop. You have my purse and my license. I think you can figure it out."

"Might be late," he said, his tone full of innuendo.

"You might get shot."

This time he laughed. "Not too late."

Chapter 12
BJ

BJ took three pills for the dull throb in her head and studied the silk-screened Allen Iverson tank top. Over black leather pants and toeless slip-ons, she knew she looked good but not like she was trying too hard. After all, she did have a mild concussion.

In the mirror, she looked into her own eyes and tried to capture the reason for her internal disquiet. Officer Riggs unsettled her. He'd been her challenger and her rescuer. He was responsible for her tender physical state and for the bruising of her moral ego. So why was she trying so hard? To show him that she was a fair person? Riggs owed her an apology and she wondered if she'd ever get one.

While she'd been lying on the floor of the Underground, she'd experienced a moment of vanity—not about her shirt being ripped, but because her abs were sucked in and he could see the lower rung of her ribs.

Only a woman, she thought as she made her way slowly down the stairs and into the kitchen. She'd planned on fixing something to eat, but she'd slid onto the mahogany barstool, turned on the TV, and watched Bernie Mac talk to America, when the doorbell rang.

Butterflies bounced in her stomach but she toughened up,

walked to the front door, and pulled it open. Riggs stood on the steps of her half-million-dollar home looking like the bum she'd met earlier that day. Her insides gurgled.

"Hello," he said.

"Hey. Come in." She recognized the pang in her chest. She was still a little afraid of him.

BJ moved through her house, hypersensitive to its flaws, even more to its grandeur. The high-priced objects she'd collected over the years were scattered like teardrops on a black wax finish, obvious in their uselessness.

Keiko Riggs didn't make worthless small talk, no banter to put her at ease, yet she led him into her home, her life, anyway. He trailed close enough for her to be able to smell his clean, masculine scent, which contrasted with his tattered clothing. Riggs was a breathing oxymoron.

If he hadn't been wearing the awful clothes—she slid onto the stool and closed her eyes.

"You aren't going to pass out on me, are you?"

"That would be too easy, wouldn't it?"

Dark brown eyes met hers. "Nothing worth having is easy," he said.

BJ didn't agree. Some things didn't have to be hard. "I'm more optimistic."

He let the difference lie between them. "I've been homeless today. Can I get a drink?"

The reminder nudged her into the uncomfortable space of their first meeting, and the reason for his presence. But she didn't feel like fighting. "What do you want?"

"Beer?"

She got up and served him, moved two spaces with her bottled water, sat down, and drank.

"What did the doctor say about your head?"

"I'll live."

The bottle stopped halfway to his mouth as he regarded her.

Then he drank. A pull from the long-neck Sam Adams made the rock in his throat go down and up in one slow, exaggerated movement.

BJ rolled her eyes.

"You're angry with me."

"Yes," she said.

"You couldn't just say that?"

"I have a concussion because of you. And then you judged me because I didn't want to give *you*—who aren't really what you pretended to be—money."

He smiled. "If I'd been a real bum, would you have given me anything?"

"No."

"Okay," he said. "I was trying to keep you safe. Harassing you for money was part of the job."

"You knew who I was. You targeted me," she said, afraid she sounded as vulnerable as she felt.

"Not unlike a criminal. A real one." He gestured at the sliding-glass screened door and she gestured with her chin that she didn't care if he looked.

"Basketball court?" he asked.

BJ didn't say anything for a moment, waiting for her brain to process the shift in conversation. He flipped on the wall switch and the outside lights flickered on. "Do you mind?"

"Yes, I mind."

"You're uncomfortable," he acknowledged. "Can we sit outside so I can apologize?"

She'd almost given up on that one fleeting hope. Something in her wanted to give him a chance. From an indoor remote, she activated the retractable bleachers and on low, the audio announcer of the last home game she'd played in.

"This is very cool," he said as he stepped out of her home and into her favorite space.

The athlete in her wanted him to love her toy. The feminist in her railed at her broken self-esteem barometer.

He walked the perimeter of the court, taking in every inch. From time to time, he'd chuckle at the announcer's excited cry of "And she scores!"

BJ wouldn't follow him, but sat on the court floor, her back against the bleachers. He finally sat down a couple feet from her. "I should have protected you better. I'm sorry."

After all he'd put her through, his admission lessened the raw vulnerability she felt. She leaned her head back with her eyes closed and under the May sky, forgave him. His gaze caressed her, but she wouldn't acknowledge him. Now they were even.

He sipped his beer and she drank her water. "How old are you, Riggs?"

"Thirty-five. You?"

"None of your damned business." She laughed when he started coughing. "Are you married?"

"Divorced, one daughter. You?" he asked, accepting her shift from what happened earlier to what was happening now.

"None of the above."

"Really?" He seemed genuinely surprised. "No secret teenager running around? No baby-daddy drama?"

"Not me."

"You must have been a good girl."

"Still am." The thunderstorm in her head rolled on. "Where's my stuff?"

He made regretful noises and pulled the objects from the inside of his coat. "An inventory slip is enclosed."

She took the clear plastic bag and gazed at the contents. "Thanks."

"It's all there," he confirmed.

"I trust you."

"You shouldn't."

BJ raised her chin a little. "Why not, Riggs? You're an anomaly, man. A mirage. A fake river to the thirsty."

He started laughing. "I don't know about that."

"Then what do you know?"

"A lot. Like your head is hurting and I should be going."

He felt the sensual tug between them but BJ wasn't going to make the first move. He came all this way to her house. The least he could do was act like he wanted to be there. "You came all this way to drop off a shoe and a purse, and have a beer? That's one expensive drink." Her meaning caught in the wind.

"Life is complicated," he supplied.

She translated: He had someone. "Then you'd better not be late."

"Please," he said, half exasperated, "tell me what you really think."

"What do I lose by telling you the truth?"

"I am the truth."

A war of words stirred inside her. "Whose truth?"

"I'm here, aren't I?"

Did he think she ought to leap for joy?

"Why'd you come over here dressed like that?" she asked him, bursting the last balloon of discomfort.

"Got a problem with it?"

"Frankly, yes. You're trying to prove something else at my expense. I live in a nice neighborhood."

"People dressed like me don't deserve to travel outside the city limits into nice neighborhoods like this?"

"Homeless people can go anywhere they want. You're not homeless, Riggs, unless I missed something between getting baited for a crime and actually becoming the victim of one."

"But you'd prefer I dressed better?"

"Yeah. Just as I'm sure you appreciate other people's good hygiene. That's one of the unspoken rules of life. If I showed up at your apartment drunk, I don't think you'd have a problem telling me not to disrespect your home."

"You're right. But why I got to live in an apartment?"

BJ could visualize her life with this man. A constant battle to have a conversation that didn't end with her wanting to beat him up. "How long have you been divorced?" she asked, ignoring his question.

"Eighteen months. How long have you been without a man?"

"Seven." He was too much for her. "Time for you to go."

He looked at his watch. "It is that time."

Walking off the court, he made sure the bleachers were fully stored before dousing the lights and securing the back door.

BJ led him through the foyer. Darkness had descended, and the shiny street bulbs provided a shroud of blue light, enough for them to regard each other.

"You won't be ashamed to let your neighbors see a raggedy man leaving your place, will you?"

"I expect several to call and make sure I'm okay. It's called looking after the people around you."

"I guess I've been put in my place."

His fingers played along the door handle. Why the hell wasn't he leaving? He'd worked her headache into a frenzy. With the bass-line beat playing in her head, BJ knew she didn't want to get to know Riggs better.

"Thanks for returning my stuff. I hope this wasn't too out of your way."

"I wanted to see you again."

"Oh." She waited for more. When none came, she flipped the handle and the door parted from the frame. "Good night."

"I'll call you sometime, if that's okay?"

"So we can argue? I don't think so."

He didn't take her rejection hard. He laughed. For the first time since they met, he didn't fluster her.

"Good arguments end with good making up."

God help the stirring of attraction in her belly. "I like my life without the drama. So you can save the arguing and insults for the street. That crap isn't welcome in my home."

"That mouth," he said. "Good night, BJ."

Before she could stop him, he pulled her into his arms and locked her lips in a soul-stirring, deeply promising French kiss. Seconds later they broke apart.

"I'll call you."

"Okay."

He went outside and she could hear him talking to someone. Then the door was pushed open all the way.

Quita stepped in and locked the door. "Damn, he laid you out with that kiss."

BJ silently agreed. "How long were you out there?"

"Long enough to know that timing is everything. He's a superfine man, but he had to go."

"When you walked in," she confessed, going up the stairs, "I was hoping you were him."

Quita made a sympathetic noise. "Ain't love grand?"

"I'm not in love with him."

"Yes, you are."

"No, I'm not."

"Yes, you are."

BJ got to her closet, pulled on her pajamas, and crawled into bed. The second her head hit the pillow, drowsiness claimed her. "No, I'm not."

Quita's "We'll see," echoed in her sleep.

Chapter 13
Ebony

Ebony pinched the phone between her head and shoulder, talking to BJ and Quita, as she reviewed notes Stan had left regarding new hires. This had been the last action item on her agenda, but Stan had moved it up. She sipped her Starbucks latte and mustered up her nerve. "Are we still going to see the Gigolo dancers?"

"Why are you suddenly so hung up on that?" Quita demanded.

Ebony shrugged self-consciously. She'd been thinking it for over a week, scared to bring it up. Every time she heard the commercial, a thrill ran through her. Maybe it was just something she had to see one time to get out of her system. "It might be fun. We haven't gone out in a while."

"When are they performing?"

"Tonight. If you're interested, I'll find out the info and e-mail it to you."

"If I feel better, I'll go with you, Ebony," BJ said, and Ebony silently thanked her.

"I'll see what I can do," Quita said noncommittally.

Ebony, feeling happy now, returned to the conversation. "BJ, the cop came to your house?"

"After I got in from the doctor. Teresa took me."

Was that comment meant for her? "Did I ask who took you?"

"No, but I thought I'd head it off at the pass."

"Will you let her tell the story, Ebony? I've got to get back to sleep," Quita said.

"It's ten in the morning," Ebony snapped.

"So?" Quita retorted. "I'm still recovering from my drunk from the other day."

"I bet you won't do that again," BJ said.

"You ain't never lied. Anyway, back to superfine Riggs."

"He had a beer and we sat on the court talking. There's nothing else to tell."

"You drank?" Ebony cross-checked the papers in her hand with the information on the computer.

"Yeah, water. He didn't stay long."

"You're the only woman I know who can give a man a hard-on while sitting on your basketball court," Quita piped in.

"Shut up, you slut," BJ laughed. "He didn't have a hard-on."

"When I saw him, he was tilting up."

BJ giggled softly. "You're a terrible liar."

"Nobody had to invite me." Now Ebony was annoyed. They were always excluding her. Here she was trying to make their evening fun, and they were doing things without her. Even to the point where she'd wanted to stay with Quita the other night while BJ had been ready to go. Only an hour after Quita had been put to bed.

"We didn't plan to get together, Ebony," Quita said loudly. "She needed someone to wake her up every few hours and I was nearby. Besides, we can do shit without you."

"Well, if you don't want to be my friend—"

"You are so juvenile! It's called 'get a life,' " Quita snapped.

"I have one." Ebony hated arguing, but she'd been feeling neglected. When they'd met at the investment class two years ago, BJ and Quita took to each other as if they'd known each other from way back. But not to her. She'd had to keep calling them until they'd warmed up and finally accepted her. But she felt as if she'd been trying to catch up to them for years.

"I'm hanging up." BJ didn't even sound as if she cared. "You two are worse than children."

"I'm not dealing with this crap. We ain't her man," Quita cut in. "Ebony, You're always whining or complaining about something. If there's a negative side, you find it."

Ebony's emotions swung past bravery to panic. She didn't want to ruin her relationship with her only friends in the world.

She was doing what her mother had done all her life. Pushing people away. "Look, I'm sorry. It won't happen again. BJ, you still there?"

Ebony prayed that BJ still wanted her around.

"Quita's right," BJ said, her voice weak. "Just back off a little."

"Okay! Can we drop this?"

"Fine," BJ said.

Nervous, Ebony didn't wait for Quita to respond. "So, is the cop your date for the week?"

"Why not? We did end up hanging out for a few hours."

"Was he still dressed like a bum?" Ebony hoped she sounded interested. She didn't know she'd been suffocating her friends.

"Yeah, he wanted to make his point that the homeless need compassion."

"So he's out busting the ones that beg—aggressively," Quita retorted. "That makes no sense at all."

"I didn't think so either. But to hear him explain it—I don't know. He made me think about—stuff."

"Stuff?" Ebony repeated.

Of the three, BJ was the expressive intellectual. She didn't flaunt her intelligence until someone said something too stupid for her to pass up. Then she was worse than a college professor. That's why she was good for the investment club. She knew a little something about everything.

"Riggs challenged me to think about things in a different way. *He* was different. I can't think of a better word for him."

"In a good way?" Quita asked.

BJ sighed. "No, well, yeah. He isn't a serial killer, but he set me up. Then he brought my stuff back. He's nice and then he's difficult. Before he left, I wanted him gone. After he left, I wanted him back. It's hard to explain."

"No, it's not. He used you to further his cause and then criticized your reaction. You were vulnerable and that's not cool, BJ," Quita said. "If you get with him, he'll always be critiquing you, and you won't ever get to be who you really are."

"Maybe," BJ agreed, "but there's something about him."

"You're thinking about him in that way?" Ebony couldn't believe her ears. The guy had gotten her mugged.

"Every woman has that billy-club-carrying caveman in mind when she meets a guy," Quita supplied in that all-knowing way of hers. "If he's scrawny, independent strong women aren't interested."

Stan's voice echoed in the hallway and Ebony tried to place the other male voice with him. The closer they got, her stomach began to cramp. "Girls, I gotta go."

"Where the hell are you going in the middle of our conversation?" Quita demanded.

"Stan's coming."

"Tell him you're on a break," Quita said.

"He's got someone with him. I think I know the guy." She looked around for somewhere to go, but was trapped between her desk and freedom.

"What's going on, Eb? You sound scared," BJ said, concerned.

Ebony ducked under her desk, but knew she couldn't stay there. "I met this guy a few weeks ago."

"You slept with him?" Quita made it sound unconceivable.

"No! I threatened to burn him with some hot coffee," she whispered.

"Why the hell would you do that?" Now Quita really sounded mortified.

"I thought he was following me."

"Well, was he?"

Ebony sighed again. "Only to give me something I'd forgotten at Starbucks."

"You're really crazy. Do you hear me?" Quita demanded.

BJ snickered.

Her eyes burned and she wiped them. "I thought I was in danger."

"Just apologize, Ebony," BJ said softly. "What's his name?"

"Boyle Robinson."

"Yuck," Quita snorted, laughing. "Why is he there?"

Ebony finally found his new hire paperwork at the bottom of the stack. "Stan just hired him as the warehouse supervisor." The men were almost upon her. "Call me later about the Gigolo thing."

"I'm going to rest for the remainder of the day," BJ said.

"I have to work." Quita didn't even sound sorry. Ebony hid her disappointment. Hadn't she gone out with them the last two times they'd asked her? But now that she'd pissed Quita off, neither wanted to hang with her.

"Call us later," BJ said, and Ebony hung up.

"Ebony!" Stan always talked in an over-the-top voice when he wanted to impress someone. To her, he was just loud.

"This is Boyle Robinson, the new manager of the distribution center. Boyle, meet my loyal and efficient assistant, Ebony Manchester."

Boyle flinched when their eyes met, but his eyes remained cold and unforgiving. Ebony felt as if she'd been dropped into a vat of mud. "Pleased to meet you." She extended her hand.

He raised his hand and scratched his temple. "Have we met before?" he asked.

Her hand just hung out there. He suddenly reached out, grabbed it, and applied an intensity just short of pain. "No, I don't think so."

"A week ago." His eyes narrowed as he glared at her. "Over a let—"

"Coffee," she burst in, yanking her hand back. "Was that you?" she said, her voice tremulous. Silently she begged him not to reveal the fact that she'd been reading Stan's letter when they'd met. But he wasn't giving in. His gaze said he wouldn't, ever.

Stan stood there grinning like a fool, oblivious to the undercurrent of war that had been declared the moment she and Boyle came face-to-face. "You look so different." Ebony tried to sound complimentary. "I couldn't place you."

"Same guy. Different suit." He turned to Stan. "Where can I find office supplies? I'll need stationery and envelopes." He kept baiting her.

Stan clapped him on the back. "Glad you're anxious to get started. Just give Ebony a list of supplies, and she'll bring them right on over. She can stay late if you need her to set up your computer. The furniture is portable if you want to give the room your own special touch." Stan shook his head from side to side as if doing so made him cool. "She'll verify that you're networked, and then show you how to set up your voice mail, e-mail, etcetera. She'll give you all the paperwork you need to complete to keep Uncle Sam happy, and, hell"—Stan laughed loudly—"whoever else wants a piece of you. What else, Ebony?"

"L-license and credit card."

"Right," Stan said. "No, Social Security card." He laughed jovially. "Women always have shopping on the brain. Anyway, Boyle, glad you're here. Welcome, and please don't hesitate to call me if you have any questions. Otherwise, I'll place you in the very capable hands of my assistant."

Ebony rubbed her disrespected hands together.

"Stan, can we go back to the warehouse? I did want to run a few things by you," Boyle asked, snubbing her.

Was he going to tell him about the letter?

"Uh, Stan, I need to talk to you," Ebony said, in her most official voice.

"In a minute, Ebony." How could Stan dismiss her? She was the one who kept his butt out of the fire. Ebony wondered how he would feel if that letter mysteriously showed up at his house? Then he'd be begging for her help.

"Do you need me right now?" he said to Boyle.

"If you're available."

"Sure thing. Ebony, hold down the fort."

"Sure," she murmured. "No problem."

Why did Boyle have a vendetta against her? She'd made an honest mistake, but did he have to ruin her career? She didn't have a degree to fall back on, and fourteen years at one company wasn't enough to get her to the next pay level at another company. She needed this job.

She tried to focus on work, but by five o'clock, Ebony's nerves were shot. She didn't wait for Stan to come back from the warehouse. She packed up and left. If she were going to get fired, tomorrow would be soon enough.

Inside her car, she sat with the air blasting. It was still daylight and the last thing she wanted to do was go home. She'd already annoyed Quita, and BJ was sick, so going over to their houses was out. She didn't have any other friends.

At the moment, Ebony hated herself. In a city of three million people, she was practically friendless.

She started her car and sat in midtown traffic listening to X-106. The disc jockey sounded too happy. *"We got the black Gigolo dancers performing tonight, so ladies get your dollar bills and come on out for the party of your life. See you at X-tasy."*

She turned the car into the Quik Trip gas station.

Ebony considered the hundred dollars in twenties she'd earmarked for the investment club and hopped out. She filled the tank and bought some crackers and a Coke. Then she pulled her makeup from an insulated lunch bag, turned up the air conditioner, and started the careful application.

No, she wasn't ever going to be a model, but she'd at least moved from invisible to blasé. Maybe tonight she'd graduate to interesting. Besides, she needed a date for this week, and one of the black Gigolos would hopefully fit the bill.

Maybe she needed to be more like Quita and BJ. Not so serious and more of a good-time girl. Well, she had tonight to enjoy herself. Nothing about tomorrow was promised.

Chapter 14
Quita

BJ picked up the ringing phone and said, "You didn't have to go off on Ebony like that."

"Yes, I did. She's driving me fucking crazy." Quita adjusted the sleep mask and tracked Jimmy's movements. He'd dropped by out of the blue, and had talked his way into her bed. Normally, she wouldn't have let him in, but he gave good lovin', and today she'd needed to be needed.

Quita suspected he had a full life elsewhere; he hadn't answered her last two calls, but she made herself not care. Oddly enough, that kept him coming back for more. Today he was useful, but she'd have to get rid of him.

Today she was going to take another home pregnancy test.

"What are you looking for?" she asked him.

"Nothing," BJ said.

"A movie," Jimmy answered.

"Who was that?" BJ asked.

"Wanna see *Deliver Us from Eva?*"

"Who's talking to you, Quita?"

The simultaneous conversations jarred Quita's nerves. "No, I don't want to see a movie. I'm sleepy." He'd kept her up all night after she'd left BJ's.

"BJ, I'm talking to Jimmy, who's a morning person, and who's going to have to take his awake ass somewhere else if he wants to watch a movie." He ignored her and started the fireplace, although her bedroom was always kept at a cool seventy-two degrees. What touched the only sentimental bone in her body was that he knew she liked making love in front of the fireplace.

"Jimmy from the club?" BJ fairly screeched.

"Careful, your head. Yeah, him."

"Didn't the doctor say you should cool it?"

"Yeah, but hey, what have I got to lose?"

"You haven't seen your cousin Ivy yet, have you?"

"No."

"You're not going to?" BJ's disappointment fed Quita's guilty conscience. It wasn't that she didn't want to see Ivy; she just didn't want to hear any more bad news, and she didn't want anyone else to question her judgment.

LL Cool J's monologue at the beginning of *Deliver Us from Eva* filtered into Quita's bedroom. "I plan on seeing her, maybe after my doctor's appointment next week."

She twisted, admiring Jimmy's unabashed nakedness. As shadows of firelight bounced off his bare skin, Quita wondered if she could live with a man forever. He looked good in her room. But just like the aesthetic fireplace, she and Jimmy didn't generate any real heat.

"I'm still going with you," BJ said. "This bump on my head isn't anything."

"You don't have to."

"Who you takin' with you then?"

"Now you sound like Ebony."

"Well, I'm not."

Quita hit her estrogen limit for hissy fits. "Look, I didn't say you *couldn't* come." Jimmy turned around, looking for all the world like

Sugar Ray Leonard. Her mother's friend Damaris had been a big fan of Sugar's back in the day.

Quita wondered if she was attracted to Jimmy because he made her think of the one man who'd been nice to her when she was a teenager. He hadn't been sleazy or tried to act like her daddy. Just a nice man who didn't mind givin' a kid a few dollars when her mother got stingy. And as much as her mother wanted, he hadn't been down with that uncle shit, either. He told her to call him Damaris, and she did until the day he died.

"What you thinkin' about, Quita?"

Quita hated that she hadn't stayed with BJ all night, but being with Jimmy quieted some of her restlessness. "Nothing, girl. Get some sleep, and I'm callin' you at one-thirty. If you don't answer, I'm coming by. Don't set the house alarm. Are you in the bed?"

Jimmy turned around and had that glint in his eye that never stopped turning her on. He wanted some, and instantly, she was ready.

"Yes," BJ said, "but don't come by. I'm cool. Teresa can't stop buggin' me long enough for me to pass out. Quita?"

Quita smiled at his I'm-in-the-mood dance, still wondering if his seed was strong enough to penetrate her obstacles. If so, he might be worth keeping around for a minute. "Yeah?" she answered BJ, knowing it was time to hang up.

"Leave something for the doctor to look at next week, okay?"

Quita burst out laughing as Jimmy licked from her toes to the arches of her feet. "You aren't sick if you've got jokes."

Still, as the hazy fog of desire grew, Quita could see BJ's point. She didn't want her personals to look like a racetrack. Wouldn't it be nice to go in there pregnant? She shook Jimmy from her feet and wiggled her fingers at him. He crawled higher and tangled his hands in her hair, seeking her mouth.

"Have one for me," BJ said.

"She will," Jimmy answered for Quita.

Quita heard BJ's yelp of surprise and her quick hang up. She'd apologize later.

"Quit messin' around and take care of business," she told him as he entered her.

Maybe this time. Please, Lord.

Chapter 15
Ebony

The fifteen-dollar admission into the club wasn't as high as Ebony expected. After all, the women she'd overheard talking said they'd have paid a lot more.

"Do you want a lottery ticket?" The redheaded woman inside the glass-enclosed booth gave her an encouraging smile.

"Sure," Ebony agreed. She didn't want to look like she didn't know what was up.

"Five dollars."

She swallowed her grimace. If she kept this up, she wouldn't have any left when the show started.

The woman slid a wristband, a ticket, and a form to sign through the chute. A quick perusal said she'd consent to whatever happened inside the club. Ebony signed and returned the paper. What could possibly happen in a room of two hundred women and fifteen men?

"Have a good time," the redhead said.

Ebony nodded her thanks and followed a throng of women who trolled the round tables, vying for the best seat. A few lucky ones got tables close to the stage, but Ebony wasn't that bold. She just wanted to be in the room with the action.

The tide swept her toward the stage, and she stepped out of the crowd at a table with a special bachelorette party flag in the center. She pulled out the chair and was eyed.

"Were you holding this seat for someone?" Ebony tensed for the rejection of the six women at the table. If they were intent on embarrassing her, she'd move now. Her feelings had been bruised enough for one day.

"You beat her to it, so it's yours."

A mocha-colored sister wearing a crisp cream-colored suit gestured for her to join them. She was a sharp executive with French-tipped fingernails and a gold-and-diamond watch on her wrist Ebony knew was from Cartier. She'd seen it on eBay for ten thousand dollars.

Ebony guessed that the wedding would easily cost her entire year's salary. Damn. Some people had it made.

She gave her drink order to the waitress and relaxed.

Palpable anticipation swept Ebony into the excitement. Her Cosmopolitan arrived and she sipped, proud that she'd come this far without BJ or Quita. Normally she would have frowned upon this type of entertainment, it *was* almost pornography, but date night seemed to have relaxed her inhibitions.

The woman on Ebony's left tapped her wristband. "First time?"

Ebony nodded. "Yours?"

"Girl, no. I'm Jessie."

"Ebony."

"It's her first time," Jessie told the other ladies at their table. Sly smiles jacked up their mouths.

As the waitress passed, the woman in the business suit whispered and pointed to Ebony. The waitress glanced at her, nodded, and walked away as music pumped through invisible speakers.

"What'd she tell her?" Ebony shouted over the bass thumps.

"That you're a Gigolo virgin."

"Oh." Ebony didn't know what to say. "Does that mean something?"

"Could. Just go with the flow," Jessie advised. The lights dimmed and a roar from the crowd filled the air.

Five chords of the Atlanta Hawks theme music pulsed through the air, and the women went wild as a dancer descended from the ceiling on a rope. Ebony watched in stunned fascination as he worked his body into a glistening sweat, while shedding one piece of clothing at a time. By the time he got down to his Speedo-type underwear, she was clapping and laughing with the rest of them.

Suddenly the room was overrun with young, muscular, beautiful men. Class and sophistication flew out the window as her tablemates screamed and squealed and flapped their dollar bills. Ebony remembered hers and dug into her purse. Being here was as close to having sex as she'd been in a while, so she was going to enjoy every minute.

The men danced on stage, in pairs, on tables, and in women's faces until Ebony forgot to be embarrassed. This was the best time that she'd had in forever.

One Cosmopolitan later, she was feeling no pain and her libido begged for satisfaction. Just when she thought she couldn't take any more, another Cosmopolitan arrived and she started to drink it when she was shoved against her chair and buckled in with a seat belt.

Her arms and were held at her sides by the belt, and she couldn't move anything except her head. She looked down. She hadn't noticed the belt fixtures on the side of the chair before.

"What's happening?"

Everyone cheered when a dancer named Gigolo Tush landed in Ebony's lap. His taunt legs straddled hers.

Her breath caught as she followed his copper thighs up to the weighty package in her lap, over a slender waist, rippled chest, and muscular throat to the most handsome face she'd ever seen up close.

Ebony fell in love. Then she started screaming.

The crowd cheered.

"I just found myself a vir-gin," he sang. His voice boomed off the walls and he put his arms around the back of her chair until she was flush against his chest.

The women in the club hooted like men.

"Do we do virgins, ladies?" he asked, holding the word forever.

"Did she consent?" They screamed.

He looked at her. "Well?"

Ebony tried to open her mouth but it wouldn't work. So she did the next best thing. She nodded dumbly.

The women roared.

An African beat of music pulsed and he started bouncing on her lap, pumping her body into a helpless frenzy. He used every inch of the table and her chair to entice her.

Jessie and the woman on Ebony's right got up so he could brace his feet on their chairs and pump his well-endowed package close to her face. He never actually touched her, but Ebony couldn't believe that she strained forward so he could.

He landed back in her lap and pushed his chest into her face. "Bite, beautiful."

She clamped her teeth on his white pirates shirt and when he flipped backward onto the table, the shirt was torn from his chest. The remains stayed in her teeth and lap.

The women in the club went wild.

Tush was bare-chested and sexy as hell when he undid the first button of her blouse and stroked her neck with his breath and the tiny tip of his tongue.

"Oh no," she cried weakly. She had the smallest boobs in the world.

The music faded a bit. "What's that, baby? You won the lottery. You don't want the jackpot?"

"Yes. Yes!"

The music increased and women screamed as he undid two more

of her buttons. He shucked the black dancer pants he'd been wearing, and stood before her in all his bare-assed glory—and a G-string.

She couldn't help but scream and bounce in her chair.

Her hands fluttered at her sides, but she was bound for a reason. If she could have gotten her hands on him, the bouncers would have had to get surgical tools to extricate her.

Suddenly, he spun her chair. Ebony felt herself falling and when she chanced looking again, she was faceup on the floor, still latched to the damned chair.

Tush's hands were on her thighs and then he moved them up.

"Whoa," she screeched.

The women in the club encouraged him by clapping and chanting, *"Do it. Do it."*

Tush dragged his hands higher on the outsides of her legs, skimmed under her skirt, and before she knew what was happening, he yanked.

Ebony screamed as her sensible Naturalizer shoes flew off, and Tush relieved her of her stockings.

He danced over her, around and on top of her, and all she could do was feel the desire, and absorb it.

He teased her mercilessly, until she was begging him to love her, along with two hundred of her now closest friends.

Tush wasn't finished. He hooked his hands between her chest and the seat belt and pulled her up slowly.

Finally, he was in her lap again.

Weak and sweaty, Ebony grinned like a fool. "That was wonderful."

"Tell me if it gets better."

He took his torn white shirt, wrapped it around her neck, and gave her the most sensual close-lipped kiss she'd ever had in her life.

Ebony was sure she'd died and gone to heaven.

Then he said, "It was good for me, was it good for you?"

The crowd erupted in renewed sensual frenzy.

"Absolutely."

He got real close to her ear. "Wait for me outside. One hour, baby."

Tush walked away with her stockings between his teeth.

Her tablemates unsnapped the seat belt, and Ebony pulled his shirt to her face and accepted his standing ovation as her own.

Chapter 16
Ebony

An hour later, Ebony anxiously sat in her car. She had to see Tush again. Her bar tab and his tip had emptied every dollar from her purse, but she knew she'd do it all over again in a heartbeat.

This moment meant everything to Ebony. She'd branched out on her own and had hit a home run. BJ would be proud—if Ebony ever told her. Ebony was especially glad Quita hadn't come because tonight Ebony had been the chosen one. When Tush had looked into her eyes, lust had been directed at her.

She touched up her makeup and prayed he'd want to continue where he'd left off.

When Tush emerged from the club and stood out front, she wasn't sure if he'd believed she'd wait for him or not. She didn't even know what to call him. She flashed her lights, and he peered but didn't approach until she drove up and rolled down the window.

"Hey, you," he said, grinning at her. "You waited."

"You told me to."

His brows furrowed for a second, then smoothed out. "Want to get some breakfast? I'm starving."

It was already eleven-thirty. She wouldn't get eight hours of sleep and she'd be tired at work tomorrow. *So,* she challenged herself. Everybody else had a personal life, why not her?

She'd never been late before without a good excuse, so if Stan had a problem, he could just get over himself. "Where do you want to go?" His grin wiped away the last of her trepidation.

"Waffle House sounds good to me. Mind if I ride with you?"

She tossed the two hundred dollars' worth of makeup into the backseat, leaned over, and unlocked his door. "Hop in."

Before he'd gotten completely in, she tried to stop smiling so hard. "I saw a Waffle House on Piedmont."

Strapped in, he scooted the seat back and reclined a bit. "That place is too crowded. I want to go someplace where we can talk and get to know each other."

"Okay." She put her car in gear and blinked back tears. This was too good to be true.

She had so many questions, but the way his fingers played a tuneless rhythm on her shoulder distracted her. When she looked over at him, he was gazing at her. "What are you looking at?"

"You. You're strong. Don't take crap off of anyone. I'm attracted to that in you."

Ebony was flattered speechless. He didn't say she was pretty. He'd have been lying. But the one trait she'd been criticized the most for was something he liked.

"What's your name?"

He started laughing. "Everybody calls me Gigolo Tush."

"Not me."

His smirk reeked of respect. "You can call me Abel."

"As in from the Bible?"

"Well," he started laughing. "I wouldn't go there. More like I hope I'm able to make love to you tonight until the break of dawn."

Ebony got wet instantly. She pulled into the Waffle House parking lot. She'd already thrown caution to the wind. As long as he had protection, she couldn't see a reason not to let him have his way. "Shall we eat first?"

"Yeah, baby. We'll eat, and then *we'll eat again.*"

Chapter 17

BJ

By five o'clock on Wednesday, BJ thought her eyes were going to roll out of their sockets. Besides the low throb that still plagued her head, she was edgy and out of sorts. She attributed some of her restlessness to the season being over and the high-maintenance players being gone, but that wasn't the crux of it.

The week was halfway over and she hadn't had a date. Drinking with Riggs didn't count. As far as she was concerned, he'd only come over to do an emotional background check and pass judgment on her life. And she could only blame herself. She'd invited him in and smeared her pride on his lips with Bonne Bell Shoutin' Sugar lip gloss. What pissed her off was that after that kiss and his casual "I'll call you," he hadn't called.

Disgusted with herself for thinking about him all day, she called Teresa. "Getting ready to head out?" BJ asked.

"Yes. Do you need something? Feeling okay?"

"I'm fine. Look, what was that thing you said your cousin was doing at Hairiston's?"

"It's called Le Flirt. You have a series of five-minute dates with men, then you score them and decide if you want to officially ask them out."

"Uh-huh." BJ's personal desperation meter confirmed her worst fear. She was lonely.

"You thinking about going?" Teresa asked shyly.

BJ didn't want to divulge the sparse details of her personal life to her secretary, but Teresa knew. Women with boyfriends went to lunch, got phone calls and rides home. BJ had none of the above. "I'm bored. I thought about stopping through."

"It's cool if you don't set your sights too high," Teresa advised knowingly. "There are lots of single women. Tons. And lots of per- petrating men, but, hey—"

BJ caught her vibe. There wasn't much chance of making a love connection, but it was better than taking her aching head home to stare at the television and occasionally check the dial tone. She popped a pain pill. "I think I'll go. Can Ebony come?"

"Sure. I'll give my cousin Sanella a call and tell her not to charge you two the twenty-five-dollar cover."

"Hey, thanks. Good night." BJ hung up and dialed Ebony at work. "I'm going to this thing tonight."

"What thing?"

"It's called Le Flirt at Hairiston's. Interested?"

"How much is it? Dating is so damned expensive."

BJ stared at the phone, not believing what she was hearing. "Tonight it's free. What have you been paying for?"

"Nothing," Ebony said too quickly. "I'm trying to save for a house. All of us aren't pulling in—" She stopped short. "I'll go."

Talking to Ebony was like driving on Georgia 400 in rush-hour traffic. You never knew what the hell was coming next.

"Good. Maybe going out and having a good time will drive one of those multiple personalities out of your system." Ebony didn't laugh. She didn't even speak. "Ebony, you there?"

"Yeah." She sighed.

"You leaving now?" BJ wondered what was wrong with her. Maybe her mother was sick.

"I'm practically out the door."

* * *

BJ sat opposite a large man who claimed he was thirty-three, but who looked at least fifty. The few strands of hair left on his head were smoothed over the crown and curled up on the other side of his head. BJ knew staring was wrong, but she couldn't look away.

Sanella discreetly flashed three fingers. "So, G." BJ used the nickname he'd given himself. "You grow up in Atlanta?"

"Born 'n' raised in Macon." His leg shook and he jostled the table. "Wha 'bout you, Sweetheart? Whatchu lookin' fo in a husban'? Cuz, I believe in gettin' right to the point! No need to waste each other's time—" He dragged out the last word. BJ couldn't believe he actually thought there was a remote possibility that he'd be a match for anyone in the building.

"I don't want to get married," she told him.

"Why you come here, den? You just wastin' people's time. I paid twenty-fi dollas to get in herr and find me somebody. My soooul mate."

Now that he was sweating, the thin strands of hair ran back across his head and dangled over his ear.

BJ grabbed her side. "My pager just went off."

"Time!" Sanella called. "Switch."

He got up in a huff, muttering about his soooul mate, and walked off.

The woman next to BJ burst out laughing. "Who does that old man think wants him, with his white-socks-wearing ass?"

BJ took a sip of Coke and held the carbonated drink in her mouth until it prickled her tongue. Yes, she was still alive. "I don't know, but it's not me."

"I'm Nisa."

"BJ," she offered.

Ebony ran over and squeezed in next to BJ. "Girl, there are some dogs in here tonight. How'd you hear about this again?"

BJ looked at her. "Teresa. What's up with you?"

"Nothing," she said, shaking her shoulder to the music. She had on blush and eye shadow that complimented each other and her outfit well.

This wasn't the same Ebony from a week ago. She'd never met this person before and BJ was curious at the cause of the transformation.

"You are acting strange. What's up with you?"

Ebony tipped her head to the side and ran her polished fingernails over the table. The in-style brown shocked BJ.

"I met someone."

"Wow." Two days was enough to turn Ebony into a different woman. "He must have hit it hard. Who is he?"

"Nobody. God, BJ, can't you just be happy for me? Are you and Quita the only ones supposed to be able to get a man?"

"I never said you couldn't get a man. You know what, this whole split-personality thing you got going is not attractive."

Nisa watched the play-by-play without a bit of discretion. "Be careful, girl, don't let him turn you out."

Ebony shrugged off the advice and a secret grin curled her lips. "It's not like that."

Sanella walked back to her perch and women scampered for their seats.

"You going back over to your assigned seat?" BJ asked Ebony.

"No. I thought I'd have better luck over here with you."

Music and voices coincided with ice clinking in glasses. The atmosphere was light and BJ decided although her last date wasn't about anything, she was having fun. She regarded Ebony. "So, who is he?"

"Aren't we getting together Sunday?"

"Supposed to." She was being impatient and secretive again. Whoever he was, he must be special.

"I'll tell you then. I don't want to jinx it. Okay?"

BJ pursed her lips. "Fine with me."

Nisa shrugged, too, as if she had some input.

BJ shifted gears. "How'd things work out with that guy at your job?"

"I didn't see him at all today. Maybe he quit."

This was the Ebony BJ knew. Not the flirty and feminine woman that flicked her head a minute ago. This mystery man was a miracle worker. BJ couldn't wait until Sunday.

"He probably already let the situation go," BJ said.

Ebony sighed. "I hope so."

"Return to your seats, ladies, or we can't continue," Sanella called into the microphone. "I know you want to see my special surprise, so hurry."

Sucking her teeth, Ebony got up. "I'm not staying much longer."

"We've only been here an hour. Give it some time."

"I've got plans," she said importantly. "Call me tomorrow."

Ebony hurried across the restaurant and back into her seat. "That girl is crazy," BJ said to herself.

"What's her name? I've seen her somewhere before."

"Ebony Manchester. You know her?"

The woman squinted her eyes. "I can't say that I do, but she looks so familiar. It'll come to me. Hey," Nisa dug into her purse and handed BJ a business card, "I travel with my job, but maybe we could have lunch sometime."

BJ reciprocated. "Sounds like a plan."

"Ladies," Sanella called to get everyone's attention. "Help me welcome the handsome, single men from the one four who hold it down every night to keep our streets safe. Meet the finest hunks of the Atlanta Police Department and the Atlanta Fire Department!"

Women screamed as the cops and fireman strolled in. BJ's heart raced. What the hell kind of luck did she have?

"Will all the men assemble in the center?" Sanella called. The floor filled with all the single men in the club. The temperature rose. "Ladies, you know the rules, the men have their pick. Now!"

The floor emptied and seats filled. BJ didn't glance up until she felt legs next to hers beneath the table. She lifted her head.

"I'm Danny," the handsome man said. "What's your name?"

"BJ." She took in a deep breath and exhaled slowly.

The man across from Nisa got up abruptly and walked out of the club. "He's gay," she told them. "I guess it was news to him."

"Oh," was all BJ could say.

Nisa sat quietly, watching the rest of the activity in the room, as Danny scrutinized BJ. "How tall are you?"

She frowned. "Why?"

"Just wondering. Five ten?"

"No."

"Six feet?"

"Why?" she demanded.

"Just asking."

"Well, ask something else."

"What do you do for a living?"

"Public relations. You?"

"Atlanta Fire Department."

"You're the whole thing?" BJ asked, annoyed.

"What?" he asked, clearly not into her.

"You're the whole fire department, or are you a fireman?"

"What you think?"

"Switch!"

"Thank you!" BJ exclaimed.

Nisa started laughing. "That was painful to watch."

"Now!" Sanella bellowed.

BJ saw Riggs coming and tried to fix her gaze elsewhere. The lighted dance floor provided a backlight for his sexy stride in his lightweight linen pants, a silk shirt, and brown Kenneth Cole shoes. She held her breath for the longest moment until he sat down—across from Nisa.

Another man sat down across from her. "Hi, I'm Tim."

If BJ had a type, he was sitting before her. Rugged and strong, the man had biceps for days as well as legs that stretched alongside her long ones under the table. The thrill she felt died, knowing she was an arm's length from Riggs, although she refused to look at him.

"I'm BJ. Nice to meet you. What do you do, Tim?"

"I'm a systems engineer." He smiled. "Boring work to you, I'm sure."

"No," she said. "I'm sure everyone needs a systems engineer at some point in their lives, right?"

They laughed. "How about you?" He leaned forward.

From the corner of her eye, BJ noticed Riggs noticing her, but she could also hear Nisa working to keep his attention.

"I work in public relations." BJ's eyes burned, she wanted to look at Riggs so bad.

"Would I know any of your clients?" She had to commend Tim for asking. Most men's eyes glazed over once she got to the word "relations."

"No," she said. Telling a man she worked for the Hawks was like feeding candy to a baby. Once they knew, they wanted the perks, and when things ended between them, they still wanted the perks. Now she rarely told anyone. "I broker deals between vendors," she added so as not to seem too mysterious.

"That sounds important," Tim said, just as Riggs reached out and touched her hair.

"How's your head?"

She yanked away. "What do you care, Riggs?"

"You two know each other?" Nisa asked, shocked.

BJ leaned away from Riggs's hand, which he'd possessively left on the table.

Tim and Nisa watched them closely. "Barely," BJ said.

"Intimately," Riggs contradicted.

"You're still a liar," she told him.

"I wasn't on top of you Monday?"

If BJ hadn't been caught off guard, she wouldn't have laughed. "Switch!"

Tim gave BJ a level stare.

"It's not what you think. He's a cop and when I got mugged, he saved me from the guy." She slid her business card across the table, hoping Tim would take it just to put Riggs in his place. Tim seemed like a genuinely nice guy. Someone she would have liked to get to know, under different circumstances. He glanced at the card and then at her. "Up to you," she said.

He left it on the table and walked away, and Nisa walked out after him.

Riggs slid over, grinning.

The switch ended and the chatter resumed.

"Asshole," BJ said quietly.

"You like my ass or I wouldn't still be sitting here."

"*Arrogant* asshole," she rephrased, drinking in the sight of him. Cleaned up, he was finer than any man she'd seen that night. "Where's your uniform? I didn't get the impression that you changed often."

He grinned and pretty white teeth flashed. "It's getting dry-cleaned. Baby, bums have standards, too."

BJ remembered them vividly. "You said hello, so your duty is over. You can go now."

The waitress stopped and Riggs placed a drink order. "What are you having?" he asked BJ.

"Nothing."

"Bring her whatever she had."

BJ ignored Riggs. She didn't need his charity. BJ got ready to make her grand exit, but didn't see Ebony. Typical. When she needed to be saved, her girlfriends were never around. Riggs looked around to see what she was looking at. BJ lost the battle to be silent. "Didn't you come here to find a woman who's going to give you a good time?"

Riggs burst out laughing. "You're joking, right?"

"No."

"Why are you still mad at me? I already apologized." His smile vanished, and he had the nerve to look vulnerable.

Their drinks arrived. Riggs flipped a ten onto the tray, and the waitress walked away.

Anger at his audacity drove BJ into a confrontation. "What makes you think you're so special that I'd spend a moment being mad at you? To be mad you have to care, and I don't know you enough to care."

He spun his Sam Adams in a slow circle and didn't fight back.

BJ got her purse and was past his chair when he wrapped his fingers around her wrist. "Say it again."

"I don't—"

His fingers tightened on her wrist and she couldn't finish.

BJ pulled her arm away and walked out of the club.

As BJ drove through the streets of Stone Mountain, Georgia, each mile took her closer to home. White headlights bounced off the back of her Benz, blazing a path to inevitability.

When she made the final turn onto her block and Riggs didn't, old insecurities crept in and started pointing fingers. But BJ didn't bow to the emotions. She kept driving. She knew her way home. When her feet hit the concrete slab, Riggs was beside her.

"Take my hand," he told her in a way that offered silent promises. But she couldn't.

"I don't know about you. You make me"—she tried to find the right word—"uncomfortable."

Riggs didn't answer, but he didn't withdraw his hand.

"How do I know you won't hurt me again?"

"I have no way of knowing that."

Riggs was fire and she didn't want to get burned. He tipped her chin up and his eyes relayed a promise. He finally said, "Never that way. Ever."

She was out of the car and in his arms, their mouths joined so quickly, he bumped into the trash can behind him. Riggs's head snapped up. "Ow." He chuckled. "You bit my lip."

"Let me see." BJ loosened her hold on him, but he stayed with her until her back was against the open doorframe of the Benz.

"I'm fine." He let her go just enough to look into her eyes. "Might be a bumpy ride." He urged her legs wider to accept the mold of his presence.

His honesty seduced her into wanting him more. She tabled her objections, focusing instead on how he made her feel.

She wasn't sure they'd make it up to her bedroom, but somehow, that seemed okay with a man like Riggs. "Make it worth my while."

Riggs's mouth moved toward hers. "I plan to."

Chapter 18

Quita

The stick was blue.

Disappointed, Quita tossed it into the garbage can. She'd taken the same test two days in a row with the same result. Maybe Doctor Tate had been right after all.

She showered and lathered her hair. Thursdays were always light days. Maybe she'd cut out of work early, and she and BJ and Ebony could go barhopping.

She pampered herself for an hour and then dressed for work.

The phone rang as she switched from her black Coach purse to Louis Vuitton. The caller ID display showed Doctor Buzu. "Hello?"

"Ms. Snell?"

"Yes?"

"This is Paige from Doctor Buzu's office."

"Yes, how can I help you?"

"We have you scheduled to see the doctor next week, and—"

The second line beeped. Upscale popped up.

"Ms. Snell?"

"Go ahead. The second line just beeped."

"Do you want to get it?" Paige asked, although the attitude in her voice said it wasn't a good idea.

"I'll call them back. What's going on?" Quita tried not to sound abrupt. Had the doctor changed his mind about seeing her?

"The doctor has an opening on Monday, and—" The phone beeped again.

"Damnit! Paige, can you hold on for a second?"

"I just have one quick question."

The line beeped again. "I have to get this. I'll only be a second." Quita clicked over. "What is it?"

"Get here fast," Carmella said with barely concealed hysteria. "Our liquor license has been suspended."

"What! Why?"

"We've been cited for serving minors. Can you come right now?"

"Ten minutes. Is the inspector still there?"

"Yes, but I'm afraid the longer I stall him, the more he'll find wrong."

"Carm, calm down. I've got to go." Quita clicked over quickly. "Paige, are you still there?"

Muzak played in her ear, and Quita banged her hand in frustration. What the hell was going on?

"Ms. Snell?"

"Yes, I'm back. What about Monday?"

"Well, I was going to offer you the open slot the doctor had for Monday, but another patient got back to us while you had me on hold."

"I said I would be right back." She had to see the doctor right away. "I'm back to waiting until next week?"

"Yes, oh, just a minute."

Paige came back before Quita could stop praying. "Ms. Snell, the doctor can see you tomorrow afternoon if you can get here by four o'clock."

Chills skated over her body. "I'll be there. Thank you."

Quita grabbed her purse and ran out the door.

*　*　*

At the restaurant, the tense silence was broken by Quita's sharp questions to the row of waiters and waitresses. "Who served liquor to a minor in my shop?"

Nobody said a word.

"We enforce every rule, every law, every code! Whoever did this had better speak up now, or everybody will be suspended until the security videos can be reviewed."

The inspector stood off to the side, his hands behind his back. Quita had no idea what he was going to do, but if her license got suspended, Upscale would fold. The public was fickle when it came to convenience.

"Carmella, call out the names of everyone who worked on May eighth. Waitstaff and bar only."

"Carmella Jerome," she said, reading her own name first. "Salvo Mariano, Trinisha Bailey, San Kiley, Jason Law, Etta Fitzsimmons, Helen Freeman, Nita Sheridan, Rocky and Bingo worked the bar that night."

Etta burst out crying. She was a single mother trying to make it. Quita knew she wouldn't break the law. She was too conscientious. Too in need of her job. "I didn't do it, Ms. Snell. You know I wouldn't."

Quita swallowed. This was the hardest part of her job. "Until further notice, you all are suspended."

Carmella's eyes were teary and filled with angry disbelief as Etta cried on her shoulder.

Quita felt for the women. "For those persons who are not guilty, I'm sorry to have to do this, but we can't allow this to go unpunished. I promise to have an answer today. I'll call everyone tonight."

They cleared the floor, and out of the corner of her eye Quita saw the liquor distributor deliveryman with her weekly order. He'd been stopped by Rocky, who Quita knew would watch every tape until they found the guilty party. He was a silent investor in the club. He stood to lose everything, too.

She approached the delivery man, whose name tag read Mark.

"We can't accept this shipment. Can you give me twenty-four hours?"

"If your license is suspended, it won't be reinstated for thirty days." The inspector put on his suit jacket.

"I realize that, but I'm going to try to work something out. Can you give me a break here?"

"Like the break you gave them? If I leave, your account with us will be suspended, too."

Quita wanted to scream. "Who are you? You're a truck driver."

"Ms. Snell?" the inspector said from behind her.

"Rocky, please?" She gestured for him to keep the driver away from her. Inspector Richard Hilton was a pale-faced man with flat black eyes and a lousy disposition.

"I have three videotapes to review. I'll watch them all right now. I will find out the circumstances and provide you with videotaped proof that Upscale is in complete compliance. We would never serve a person illegally."

"You can review your tapes, but we have witness testimony and a videotape of our own." He handed her the citation. "If by some miracle you find that your staff wasn't complicit with this act, you can have your say before the review board next month."

"Next month? I'll be out of business by then."

Her world was crashing. Everything she'd worked for was spiraling down the drain.

"That's the best I can do," he said, and walked out.

Quita couldn't stop her hands from shaking. She crushed the citation as a scream snaked up from her feet, through her body, and leapt out of her mouth.

A vase of magnolias rested on the hostess stand and she threw them against the wall. The ear-splitting crash of glass thrust her back into reality.

"Are you trying to put yourself out of business?"

Quita turned. The delivery man again? "What the hell do you know?"

"Tearing the place up isn't going to save it."

"Get out!" she raged. "Get the fuck out or I'll—"

"What?"

He was so cocky, standing in her restaurant, telling her what to do.

"Why don't you stop having your tantrum long enough to realize that you're going to be out of business because you were wrong? You treated them like subjects, not people. Had them begging for mercy and you still suspended them."

He shook his head and she felt each twist as a slap to her face. Who did this white man think he was talking to? He didn't know what he was talking about.

She'd had to take the hard-line while the inspector was here. Who knows what he would have thought if she hadn't? But he'd left anyway. Hadn't even offered to speak up on her behalf for not having any other violations.

The air conditioner kicked on, masking the hard breaths she took. "Your job is to deliver. Don't come near this floor again."

He gave her a dismissive look.

"Rocky?" she called, wanting this man gone.

"He's watching the videotape."

"Get out."

"I'm only going to say this because I like the people that work here. You were set up."

That wasn't a revelation to her. "For all I know it was you," she told him. "Are you out to run my business into the ground?"

When he didn't answer, she boldly walked past him to the janitor's closet. "This will go away. How about you?"

He slapped his thighs and she hated that she jumped. "It's your livelihood, not mine." He started down the hall.

If he didn't want her business, what did he want? "What about my shipment?"

When he turned back, she wanted to slap the smirk off of his face. "You expect me to hold it for you?"

"Yes."

"No." He pushed open the rear door and put on sunglasses that hid his eyes.

Quita ran after him. "Then what was all the talk for? You're just another obstacle to overcome."

His chuckle mocked her, but he wrote on the back of a business card and shoved it into her hand. "I'm going to do the right thing because of those girls. You can take it or leave it, so, do your thing, sister girl."

He stepped up to her and she moved. "Call the office and re-schedule, *if* you get your license back."

When he sped off, she read the slip, slammed the back door, and ran to her office.

Two hours later, Quita had BJ in her office along with Rocky and Bingo. They watched the tape together and saw the entire incident unfold. "I can't believe this was a setup." Mark, the jerk, had given her the time frame to view and he was right.

They all witnessed the waiter approach the table with a bottle of wine. From the back he could have been anyone. The Upscale camera captured him as he poured wine into the glass of a young person that couldn't have been any more than twelve years old. She picked it up and drank.

"He knew what he was doing and he tried to hide."

A man strolled into view, a nice knit shirt covering amazing bi-ceps. *Mark.* He sat at a table away from where the waiter stood in clear sight of all the happenings. She'd never noticed him before. Never knew he'd come to Upscale after hours. He'd seen it all.

BJ squinted at the grainy screen. "I still can't tell who the waiter is."

Quita took charge. "He thought he was being slick by keeping his back to the camera. No doubt he seated them this way on pur-pose. Watch." Rocky paused the video and pointed to a spot higher than the subject's head.

The mirror across the restaurant reflected his features.

"Salvo," Rocky exhaled. "Check this out." He advanced the tape, paused, then pointed again. The mirror also reflected the discreet photographer. "That's Salvo's brother. I met this dude when he came to pick Salvo up the day he was sick. I believe this tape was turned over to the commission."

Sick to her stomach, Quita tried to block out Salvo's words. Why couldn't she turn back the clock and be in bed with Jimmy, being made love to, instead of here watching her dream slowly implode? Unable to watch further, she focused on BJ. "I need to do some damage control for tonight. What do I do?"

"Open for business."

"Without a liquor license? The word will get out and that will kill us."

"It's four o'clock. Too late to get your license reinstated today. Are you prepared to take a loss on the whole day?"

Again, her stomach lurched. "I can't do that either."

"Then open. Tell your customers that you're being audited, and can't serve anything from the bar. Offer free desserts to everyone."

"I like that," Rocky agreed.

"But how do I get my license back before next month?"

BJ got up. "Quita, you have an attorney. Use him. Get your evidence before the right people and do it today and tomorrow morning. A confession would help a lot."

Bingo, Rocky's lover of twelve years, cracked his knuckles. The man rarely talked, but communicated effectively.

"We're not breaking any heads." Quita picked up the phone. "I'm going to call everyone back to work but Salvo. While they're on their way in, I'm going to have him arrested. Bingo, go lock up the bar and get some tickets out to make it look like inventory is being done. Rocky, tell the chef we're going to need triple the desserts for tonight. Help him get everything out of the freezer."

The men headed out, leaving BJ and Quita alone. "You're going to be fine," BJ told her calmly. "I'm going, but call if you need me."

"Thanks." Quita tried to hold herself together. "I appreciate everything."

"Good luck."

"Hey," Quita called, and BJ turned at the door. "The appointment was changed to tomorrow."

BJ winked. "I'm there."

Quita dialed her friend Captain Leon Hoover at the police station and relayed the incident. Fifteen minutes later he was in her office and she replayed the evidence. He promised to pick up Salvo for questioning within the hour.

Calling the staff was the hardest. Most were relieved, but Etta and Carmella refused to take her calls. Quita had to plead with Etta's sister before she came to the phone. "Etta, I'm sorry. I thought if I suspended everyone, I was being fair across the board. I know you didn't do this."

"You didn't act like it. I could tell by your eyes."

"Etta, that wasn't directed toward you."

"It was directed at all of us. Me and Carmella try to give our very best and we get suspended like we don't matter."

Silence fell between them and Quita didn't know what to say. She'd been angry, hasty even, but that had been fueled by the thought of losing all that she had in the world.

"I'm sorry," she said again. "I don't know what else to say. Etta?"

"Yes, Ms. Snell?"

The ground Quita felt she'd gained over the months with the young woman slipped away. "I understand that you're upset with me. I could have handled the situation better, but I'm not an expert. Please accept my apology, and I hope to see you for your shift tomorrow."

"Who's taking our shifts tonight?"

"No one. They're yours if you want to come in."

"It was Salvo, wasn't it?" Carmella said.

Quita's heart pounded. "Carm, I didn't know you were on the phone."

"Well?" she asked coolly.

"Yes. He's being questioned now."

"You're pressing charges?"

"I can't go into the details, but he committed a felony. Even if I didn't want to press charges, he escalated the situation when he secretly videotaped the incident in an effort to sabotage me. Us. He will be prosecuted."

"Damn," Carmella said. "That's deep. He must hate you."

These girls were young, but Quita wasn't going to let them obliterate the line.

"Justice will be served. If you're interested in working tonight, then we'd love to have you."

"Ms. Snell?" Etta said, her voice far less distant than before.

"Yes, Etta?"

"I need a raise. A dollar an hour."

"Two," Carmella corrected forcefully. "We've got kids, and tonight opened our eyes to a lot of things."

Hers, too. Quita couldn't afford to give raises. How would today's events impact tomorrow's bottom line?

But if she lost two valuable employees, how long would it take to train more good people? Forced to concede, she strove to sound authoritative. "I can go as high as a dollar. We're losing thousands tonight."

"Two." Carmella wouldn't back down. "We're good waitresses. We can go somewhere else and be treated like crap."

She'd already lost Salvo. How many others would follow?

"All right, Ladies. I'll expect you tonight. Good-bye."

Quita disconnected the call. Exhausted, she forced herself to call and retell the details to her attorney, Asher Devlin, who promised to track the legal end and get her an emergency hearing.

Quita was able to stay off the phone until Devlin called back an hour later from the precinct. His voice filled her ear. "He's singing like a bird."

Quita sighed in relief. "Why did he do it?"

"He claims you were unfair and made him go home. He wanted to show you how it felt to lose money."

"He had the flu. He'd been sneezing over the silverware." Angry heat suffused her. "I swear, if I get my hands on him—"

"Quita," Devlin said, his rich baritone as thick as his bank account. "You won. No need to continue to fight this battle."

"Are you sure you'll have a signed confession?"

"No doubt about it. The hearing," he said, before she could ask, "is at nine o'clock tomorrow morning. Don't be late."

"I'll be there early. Bye."

Just as she hung up, the phone rang. "Upscale?"

"Marquita Snell?"

Quita glanced at the caller ID. The *Atlanta Business Chronicle.* Surely this wasn't newsworthy. This would be old news tomorrow. "Yes, who is this?"

"I'm Doug Jackson from the BC. Were you cited for serving alcohol to minors?"

"No."

"We have a copy of the citation."

"How did you come to have that?"

"How do you think your patrons will react to the news that you serve alcohol to children?"

"My patrons know me and they know I wouldn't do that."

The second line rang and the *Atlanta Journal-Constitution* popped up on the caller ID. The third line rang. The *Atlanta-DeKalb Gazette.*

Quita lowered the phone. Salvo had set out to ruin her and she wasn't sure that even with the evidence she had, he hadn't succeeded.

Chapter 19
Ebony

A s Ebony lay beneath Abel, she tried to console him. "Maybe if we weren't in such a hurry, he would . . . it would," she floundered, "wake up."

"This has never happened before. I swear."

Hearing his lame proclamation didn't make her feel better. She hadn't had sex in over a year, and when they'd tried to make love on Wednesday night, Thursday night, and now this morning, bombs should have been blasting as far as she was concerned.

She fully expected that after she'd dropped a hundred dollars again last night to watch him perform, and endured his pleading for her to spend the night, he would make good on his promise to screw her brains out. But at the crucial moment, Abel wasn't able.

"You hungry?" he asked, rolling off of her.

"All you think about is food." Horny and befuddled, she lay in his bed with time on her hands to examine a room she'd come to hate. He touched the vee between her thighs. "Man cannot live on woman alone."

Ebony moved his hand away none too gently. "Especially when he doesn't seem fond of the dish to begin with."

Sitting up, her feet came down hard on the floor, startling her.

She'd forgotten she was so close to the matted oak-colored carpet. His mattresses were stacked three high with no frame or headboard. His bedcoverings were relatively new, and the sheets Downy fresh, but the dingy surroundings didn't inspire a desire to stay long.

She attributed his meager belongings to the short amount of time he'd been in Atlanta. It took longer than six months to establish oneself, but this ramshackle apartment he shared with two of the other dancers bordered on poverty.

Ebony gathered her clothes and started to get dressed.

"I thought we were going to play hooky?"

She fastened her skirt and smoothed it into place. "I really should go to work."

"But what will I do all day without you?"

Get a day job, she wanted to say, but didn't. When she'd mentioned it last night, he'd taken offense and explained his feelings about anything interfering with his art.

"What would you normally do without me?" she asked him.

"Get into some trouble." He grinned at her and her heart leapt. When he reached for her, she almost changed her mind.

Taking her hesitation as acceptance, he slipped his hands beneath her skirt and fondled her. Ebony didn't have a problem responding to him. Her body had been denied the presence of a man for so long, just hearing him breathe as he slept next to her bolstered her womanly soul. She was the source of contentment for a man. The power in that knowledge took her breath away.

She gripped his head, which he'd burrowed beneath the black-and-white floral polyester. "Tonight, okay?"

"What if Mr. Happy's been reassigned?" he asked, gazing into her eyes.

Ebony felt the strains of love pull at her heart. He needed her comfort. "I'll bring a surprise that he can't refuse."

Abel fell on his back, arms spread wide, his naked body a magnificent piece of art. To look at his impressive flaccid size, she'd have thought they'd have been rockin' for days. Instead, there'd been no rocks, no nothing. On her lunch break, she'd run to Frederick's of Hollywood and buy something sexy. Maybe his libido needed a shock.

She picked up her briefcase and looked around. "Abel, have you seen my purse?"

He shot up, glancing around quickly. "Maybe you left it in the kitchen."

She'd bought Chinese food last night. "I thought I'd brought it in here with me. I'll go check," she said, but Abel tugged her back.

"Let me. You know those pigs," he said, referring to his roommates. "They may have an orgy going on out there."

"That doesn't scare me. I've got the best there is." Ebony spoke the words boldly to see how he'd respond.

"Baby." His hands snaked around her waist as he rubbed his thickness against her. "Can I protect you from those pigs and go find your purse? Can I do the manly thing here, please?"

She sighed. Oh, how she'd prayed she'd meet someone who wanted to take care of her. Ebony knew she was capable of financially supporting herself, but it felt good knowing there was a man out there who wanted to nurture her emotionally.

Abel needed some work, but she could help him. They could make a very good team.

"Fine." She rubbed her rear against his fully engorged member. "Protect me from the big beasty roommates. I'll wait here."

He hurried out and she stayed in one place, glad she'd already put her shoes on. If they were going to be together, he'd have to move. This place wasn't fit for an animal.

Abel came back with a small black bag on his finger. "Looking for this?"

Ebony smiled as she took it. "Yes, thank you. I guess it's time for me to go." After she'd made all the fuss about leaving, now she didn't want to. Maybe if they had all day to explore each other's bodies, perhaps then—

"Have a good day, Ebony. I'll miss you." He planted the sweetest kiss on her lips and then on her forehead. Abel took her hand and walked her to the front door. "I'll call you on your cell phone later." She gave a quick nod before the door closed and she was on the outside, alone.

Blinking into the sunshine, Ebony hurried down the stairs and locked herself in her car. This area of town was known for being dangerous. If she and Abel were going to have any type of future together, it wouldn't start over here.

Starting the engine, she looked down and then squinted. Her shoes were two different colors.

Great. Now she'd have to stop by her house before going to work. Her mother would probably have a fit because she'd stayed out all night. But it was time for Mama to go. Time for Ebony to put her future into motion—with her man.

Maybe her mother would be asleep and she could skip the questions.

"Where the hell you been, girl?"

Ebony brushed past her mother, who looked especially grumpy this morning. Her hair hadn't been permed in months and new growth had created a thick barrier at her scalp, while the permed ends hung limply, like branches on a willow tree.

"I'm an adult, Mama. I'm living my life."

"Well, what about us? You don't have any responsibility to the two *family* members you live with?"

Ebony walked up the stairs and unlocked the door to her room. "You live with me, Mama. Not the other way around."

"You ain't never been considerate. You hop up when them two girls call like they owe you a kidney or something. I called your cell phone ten times if I called once, and you never answered."

"I don't have that cell phone anymore."

"Fine time to tell me. What if I had been sick?"

"Mama," Ebony said as she perched on her knees half in her

130

closet. "You never get sick when I'm not home, only when I'm about to go someplace. Not having my cell phone number hasn't been a problem. I don't expect it to start."

"What you sayin' chile', that I plans when I'm gone be sick? Why would I do that? It ain't like you the best company to be around. I'll bet you messin' around with something that ain't no good for you. You never did listen to me. Always to your daddy and your friends in the street. Never the one person who spent forty-eight hours in labor, bringing you here."

Ebony yanked her navy blue pump from beneath her suitcase and threw up her hands to stop an avalanche of linen from toppling onto her head.

"Mama, I've got to get to work."

Her mother was inside her room. "Look at this place," she said with contempt. "You got all types of stuff up here me and Jo could be using." She fingered the plush towels Ebony had planned to put in her mauve guest bathroom in her new house. "The rags we got ain't fit for people, let alone two healthy women."

Her mother gave her the basics in life. Not a bit more than food, clothing, and shelter. She blamed Ebony for her poor existence and wanted nothing more than to drag her down into the depression of her life. Only Ebony wasn't willing to go there. She'd seen the other side and she wanted to live on easy street. They'd had little more than threadbare towels when she was growing up and now she wanted Ebony to hand over the towels she paid twenty dollars for? No way.

Her mother eyed her private stash of shiny new kitchen appliances, anger shooting from her eyes. When she picked up the boxed handheld mixer, Ebony revolted.

"You get money every month, courtesy of the government. Why don't you buy yourself some towels?" She took the box from her mother's hand and shoved it into the overcrowded closet. "You act like I owe you something."

"You do! You owe me respect for bringing you here," Ruby Dee shouted. "You always were a selfish child. You played by yourself most of the time because other kids didn't like you."

"I played by myself because none of the kids' parents could stand *you*, Mama," she screamed back. "You haven't been happy with me a day in my life. You didn't have a baby because you wanted one. You had one so you could hold it over Daddy's head."

"You're just like your lying daddy. He went to hell for all the lies he told and you gone do the same if you don't start treating me better. It's in the commandments. They don't say nothin' 'bout honoring your child. I raised you to respect me, and by damn you will."

Ruby Dee raised her cane. Ebony shoved Ruby Dee's arm against the door. "Raise your hand to me again and I won't be the only one joining my daddy in hell. You'll be right next to me." She made sure her mother smelled her stale Chinese food breath. "Remember that power of attorney you signed when you had knee surgery, Mama? I own your life."

Her mother's eyes glittered with hate. "I was a beauty queen. I don't deserve this. Look what I gave up for you! You owe me."

"Your freedom is at my discretion. I see a nice insane asylum in your future. Just think, you and crazy Ms. Lullie, sharing a room at the state hospital."

Mentioning the woman who'd gone crazy after she'd been out drinking when her apartment burned down and her kids died in the fire had the desired affect on her mother.

Ruby Dee had scorned the woman who talked to herself and ate out of the garbage, but her mother had never once had a kind word. In Ebony's eyes, her mother was no better than the old woman. And the last thing Mama wanted was to spend her final days with a woman she'd condemned.

"Get out of my room and don't ever come back."

Her mother scurried out, calling Jo. Ebony could hear her hefty aunt coming through the kitchen one lumbering step at a time.

Ruby Dee's cries that Ebony was crazy ended in muffled condolences from her aunt, who never got into the middle of their spats. Good thing. Jo knew which side her bread was buttered on.

Already late for work, Ebony stopped for a minute and rifled through a two-inch stack of business cards and found the one to a Realtor she'd met at her church. BJ was right. She had to get out of there or someone would get hurt.

She had a couple thousand stashed away. Maybe that'd be enough. If not, she'd have to use her investment-club money.

She and Abel could make it if they pooled resources. She'd talk to him about it when he called later.

Chapter 20
BJ

"Teresa, it's BJ. It's seven-thirty, Friday morning," she said into the voice mail. "I won't be in today. I'm fine, just taking a mental health day. If you need me, I'll be at home. Bye."

"You done?" Riggs eyed her appreciatively.

"You in a rush or something?"

"Or something."

She had to give it to him, the sex had been fantastic. Him coming back last night after she'd left Upscale had been a nice surprise. Since they'd been so intimate, she'd wanted to ask the loaded question, "Do you have someone," but didn't know how she'd respond if he answered "yes."

"I have to call Quita and Ebony. If they call work and I'm not there, they'll freak out."

"Are they your sisters?"

"No."

"Why do you have to explain your actions to them?"

"Because they're my girls."

"You can't do anything without them?"

"Why are you trying to start something?"

"I'm not. My ex always had her skinny-ass sisters sitting up in

135

our house till all times of the night. We couldn't do anything without them butting in. You know what I'm saying?"

"My friends aren't like that." She left the messages anyway. "You hungry?"

"Are you cooking?"

She eyed him skeptically. "Do you cook?"

"No."

"I'll cook," she said, feeling domestic. "My specialty is omelets."

He lay back and grabbed the remote. "Cool."

She yanked the remote from his hand and put it behind her back. "If I'm cooking, then you're admiring me from the bar. Everybody has a job."

A lazy grin curved his mouth, and she was again struck by how handsome he was.

In the kitchen, she gathered the ingredients and he watched. "Why'd you get divorced, Riggs? She couldn't stand you?"

He chuckled. "You wake up with a lot on your mind, don't you?"

"Do you always answer questions with another question? You make having a conversation more difficult than a tooth extraction."

"We got divorced because we didn't know how to stay married. We had a kid. I wanted my wife to stay home. We agreed that she'd homeschool, but she wanted to work."

BJ tossed ingredients into the egg mixture. "I'd think you'd need two incomes to make it these days. You didn't want her to be happy?"

"We agreed that raising children was an important job and to do it right, someone should dedicate themselves to it full-time."

BJ whipped the eggs into a fluffy soup and poured them into the frying pan. She folded the eggs over until they were done and slid them onto the plates. "How old is your daughter?"

"Eleven."

"Smart?"

"Supersmart."

"Then you must have done something right."

He reached for the bread and put it in the toaster. "My wife and I had an agreement. She should have honored her commitment."

It wasn't just his words, but his tone that rubbed BJ the wrong way. "I guess you don't believe in changing jobs. You must have always wanted to be a detective, making"—her gaze shot to his—"moderate pay for long hours. You don't think the nature of your job might have been a contributing factor? Or it could have been your sunny disposition."

His expression didn't relay appreciation for the words she'd chosen. The toast popped up and she grabbed two slices and handed him the other two. They buttered and jellied them in silence.

Wow, great post-sex talk, BJ.

"When you make a commitment, you should keep your word. Nothing is comfortable all the time," Riggs pointed out.

BJ wasn't going to let him get away with imposing his archaic views on her. "Before this goes too far, I want to say I'm sure you both did what you thought was best, so let's change the subject."

"How would you know?" he said as he forked up food and ate.

"How would I know what, Riggs? About kids, homeschooling, marriage, or all of the above?"

"All of the above."

Defensive, BJ wiped her mouth and swallowed her food. "I don't believe you have to have been a slave to understand the pain and torment actual slaves endured. In that same vein, you don't have to have a child to know that raising one full-time *and* homeschooling are, in and of themselves, difficult."

"But you don't know firsthand." He waved her barren, marriage-less state in front of her face like a matador.

"Asked and answered." BJ got up. "I cooked, you wash. I'll be right back."

BJ escaped to her room and shut the door on her closet before she groaned aloud. What a jerk. No wonder his wife left him. He's inflexible, stubborn, and unforgiving.

She looked at herself, hands clenched at her sides, her face pinched. *Could I feel this way for fifty years?* That's like serving a life sentence in prison! Her whole body tensed. What had she seen in him? Boldness that appealed to her femininity, and the fact that he knew who she was and hadn't tried to take from her. Last night she'd wanted to be emotionally connected and they had been, but in the dusty light of this June morning, they were continents apart socially and, more important, emotionally.

How was she going to get rid of him?

The phone rang and BJ hurried out of the closet to get it. "Hello?"

"Ms. Jason? This is Fanny Margolis from the Dunwoody Hills Assisted Living Center."

"Yes, Fanny, what's going on?"

"Your grandmother fell today and was taken to Northside Hospital."

Her heart thundered. *Please don't let her be dead.* "Was she hurt bad?"

"We're a bit short-staffed today."

"She was conscious?"

"Yes, just a little disoriented."

"Could you tell if anything was broken?"

"No, but she was in pain. She was crying when she left."

Her grandmother didn't cry unless something really hurt. "Did they check her in?"

"They just left. She told me not to call you because she wanted to call you herself, but procedure—"

"You did the right thing." BJ tore through her closet and threw on a pair of slacks and a cotton top. She slammed her feet into sandals and was out of the closet when she ran into Riggs. She dumped her purse on the bed, searching for her insurance card. Finding it, BJ stuffed everything back into her bag.

"Fanny, I'm on my way to the hospital. Did anyone go with her?"

"Not in the ambulance, but the nurse's aide drove her own car over there."

"Okay, I'll call later when I know something."

BJ hung up and looked for her car keys. "I have to go. My grandmother fell down."

"This isn't an excuse to get rid of me?"

BJ focused on him. "What did you say?"

"Is this your clever way of getting rid of dates?"

The man had issues. "Riggs, my seventy-eight-year-old grandmother fell down and is now at Northside Hospital. I'm leaving to go there. You're—just leaving."

"I'll go with you."

"I'm going alone."

He dressed and BJ was angry that he hadn't been dressing while she'd been on the phone. He'd obviously been listening!

Finally he stood straight; the bed was between them.

"I'll call you later," he said.

Don't, she wanted to say, but didn't. The last thing she wanted was to engage in another discussion with Riggs.

He walked out the front door before she locked it, set the alarm, and exited through the garage. As the automatic garage door slid up, she could see him sitting in his car in front of her house.

Moron, she thought as she tore down the street. If she got lucky, she'd never see him again. But knowing Riggs, he'd just take it as an invitation to start another argument.

Chapter 21
Quita

Quita sat outside the hearing room where the fate of Upscale was being decided. Asher Devlin, LLC, was inside, doing his job for three hundred dollars an hour. She watched time slip into hour four.

Upscale was solvent, but this was putting a dent into their cash flow. She hoped for a quick rebound, but the public response would be lukewarm, since they'd been accused of wrongdoing. These days even if you were proven innocent, a good percentage of people would always believe in your guilt.

She got up, unable to sit another moment, and wondered what was keeping BJ. She'd left three messages at her house, but hadn't gotten a return phone call. That was so unlike her.

Quita wiped her face, tired.

All night she'd lain awake and replayed the events of the last two days through her head, and had come up with a hundred scenarios of how things could have been done differently.

Some of the fault lay at Salvo's feet, but her reaction had been wrong. She'd damaged some relationships, and she didn't know if they could ever be repaired. Now she was stuck. Waiting for her attorney to get back to her. Waiting for the commission to red- or green-light her financial existence. This was too much. She tried BJ again at work.

"Hello?"

"BJ! Where the hell have you been?"

"Ms. Snell, this is Teresa."

"I'm sorry—"

"No problem. Look, I just got a message from BJ that she wasn't going to be in, but—"

"She sick again?"

"No, but Dunwoody Hills left a message that Granny had an accident. BJ's probably with her. Have you tried her cell?"

Quita's eyes closed slowly. *Lord, not another thing today, please.* "No. Where's Granny?"

"The nurse didn't say. I would think Northside. They took her there the last time. You can't have cell phones on in the hospital, so I can't get through to BJ."

"I'll find her, Teresa. I'll call you back."

As much as Quita's problems consumed her, she needed to find her friend. She dialed and Ebony picked up on the second ring. "Hey, babe. I've been trying to reach you."

"It's me, Quita."

"Oh." Ebony sounded like she'd swallowed a bowl full of fish. "What's up?"

"Granny fell, and I'm at the commission hearing and can't get away right now. Can you get over there and see if BJ is okay?"

"What happened?" She sounded panicked. "What commission hearing?"

"Ebony, I need you to stay calm. Forget the commission hearing for now. Can you get to Northside and check up on BJ?"

"I'm over that way now."

"You not working today?"

"I had an appointment with a Realtor. Besides, I have forty sick days. It's time I started taking them. You okay?" she asked unexpectedly.

"When we get together, we've got a lot of catching up to do."

"All right," Ebony said, now the calming force. "I'll get the status as soon as I get there. I'm on Peachtree Dunwoody Road now."

"My cell is on," Quita said, and hung up.

She swallowed another cup of stale coffee and looked at her vibrating phone again. Jimmy. What did he want?

"Quita," she hissed.

"Good morning to you, too, sweetness. How's your day?"

"Jimmy, I'm busy right now."

"I thought I'd come over and entertain you."

"No, thanks. Look, I can't see you anymore. I've got a lot going on and you're too distracting, okay, so we need to cool it."

"What?" he said. "What the hell just happened?"

"I've got too much on my mind. I can't deal with someone who wants more of my attention."

The door to the hearing room opened. "I've got to go."

"Wait! Baby, can we talk about this?"

"This is what I want, Jimmy. Bye."

She stood up as the room emptied. Asher took his time, his big voice rumbling out of the room like a swollen river. He shook hands with everyone who passed him and Quita was glad he was on her side. He approached, his broad body dwarfing hers.

"Shall we walk, young lady?"

Quita couldn't tell his exact age, but Asher wasn't much older than her. Yet his presence dictated a level of respect that far exceeded his years.

He'd already schooled her to keep her emotions to herself, no matter the outcome. Quita couldn't tell anything as he led her through the courthouse and out into the sunshine.

"Asher?" she said, unable to remain quiet.

"You did fine. Your license is reinstated with praise from the commission for your professionalism."

"Yes!" she exclaimed, and gripped the railing as a flood of emotions hit her. Quita launched herself into Asher's arms. "What would I have done without you?"

He held her until Quita pulled away. For a quick second, she saw youthful desire in his eyes. Then it vanished. "You can pay your bill on time, and I'll be quite happy. Can I give you a lift?"

Asher was right, of course. Nothing worthwhile could develop between them. He needed a power wife and she needed a sperm donor. Two vastly different things.

"I've got my car. Thank you again."

Quita felt his eyes on her as she climbed into her Benz, started the engine, and backed out of her parking space. She drove away and caught a glimpse of him clutching his heart.

He was a perfectly good man, but she felt nothing at all for him. Quita couldn't help but wonder if her mind-set was the problem, and not her reproductive system.

Chapter 22
BJ

A firm hand on BJ's arm woke her.

"Hey," she said to Ebony, who captured her in a fierce hug. She was in a waiting room outside radiology. "How'd you know I was here?"

"You can't hide from the watchdog."

BJ grinned, too. "Quita?"

Ebony nodded and sat next to her. "How long has Granny been in X-ray?"

She struggled to see her watch. "Twenty minutes. Long enough for me to doze off." BJ rubbed her face. "God, I'm tired."

"You've had a tough week. How bad is she?"

"Right now they think her ankle is just sprained, but she's seventy-eight. They're not taking any chances. After X-ray, I hope she can go home."

"Well, thank God it wasn't serious. I—" She hesitated. "I thought the worst."

BJ patted her arm. "I did, too. Eb, she's getting old. When I got here and saw her lying in bed, I got scared." BJ tried to shake off the cloak of fear that had wrapped around her shoulders.

"She'll tell you when she's ready to die, BJ."

BJ started laughing and the pressure lessened. "You're right. She won't keep it a secret."

The door to the radiology room slowly opened and Granny was wheeled out just as Quita entered the hallway. "Granny," she exclaimed from down the hall. "You had me scared to death, old woman. Why are you playing with me like that?"

BJ stood as her grandmother's eyes brightened. "Ms. Lady," she called to Quita, "I knew it'd get you down here to see me if I shook you up a little bit. Look at what I got to do to get my girls together."

Quita leaned down and kissed Granny on her cheek in bright red lipstick. Ebony shooed Quita away and started wiping Granny's cheek with a hankie. "Lawd, I missed you girls." She looked at BJ. "You may as well get in on the lovin' now, 'cause I'm staying here a few days."

They all looked up at the radiologist, who'd witnessed the reunion in silence.

"Your doctor will explain, but she's got a broken bone. That's why they're going to observe her overnight. The ER doctor will give you the rest of the details," she said in a friendly tone. "No more shuffleboard for you for six weeks, Granny."

"I knew I shouldn't have used my foot to stop that thing, but the other team was cheating."

Too shocked to speak, BJ exhaled sharply. She fingered her grandmother's white hair.

Quita's eyes were moist and Ebony's lips were sucked in. They all waited for BJ's reaction. She tried to tell herself it wasn't serious, but that didn't stop the emotions from rushing to the surface.

"Beverly Jason," Granny said sharply. Her grandmother had never been hospitalized before. "Being in the hospital don't mean I'm gone die here. So get that look off your face. I haven't even picked out my funeral dress, so that means I'm not going anywhere anytime soon. Ebony?"

"Ma'am?"

"Drive this thing out of the way while my granddaughter gets herself together."

BJ wiped her leaking eyes, telling herself her grandmother was going to be okay.

"Ms. Lady?" she said to Quita.

"Yes, Granny?"

"Them some mighty sassy shoes you got on there. Got 'em in my size?"

Quita took BJ's hand as if she were a child and pulled her after them as they slowly trailed the radiologist, who was leading them back to the ER. "I'll give you these if you get up and walk."

Granny started laughing, a sweet tinkle that never failed to warm BJ's heart. They all giggled. "BJ?"

"Yes'm?" she said, vowing not to cry anymore.

"Ms. Lady's got more God in her than she knows. Get up and walk," she repeated. "Good Lawd." An older black man nodded his head to BJ's grandmother as he passed.

She grinned back and BJ took over pushing the chair.

"Girls," Granny said. "When I came in I saw a bunch of mighty fine men. Maybe we can pick us up a few."

"Granny," Ebony shushed. "Not if they have on gowns."

"Not if they have on the green uniforms," Quita added. "That means they're orderlies."

"Not if they're just standing around. That means they're waiting on someone, probably a wife."

Granny stopped the chair. "You three ain't never gone get married. You got too many standards. All I want mine to have is a heart and his own Social Security. The rest is negotiable."

The radiologist laughed and pointed. "You're in here. Pleasure to meet you, Granny."

"You're a sweetie, Lizette. Come by and see me. Bring candy," Granny called, and BJ pushed her chair into the room.

"You eat too much of that stuff. Let me go see how long they think they're going to keep you."

Two hours later, as Granny slept in her new temporary home, BJ eased into the hallway with Quita and Ebony.

"How did things go this morning?" BJ asked Quita as they headed to the cafeteria for a quick bite.

Ebony grabbed a banana, saw the price, then put it back.

"Long story short—" Quita paid for the banana, a Coke, two bags of chips, and an egg salad sandwich. "Our license was reinstated."

BJ breathed a sigh of relief. "That's great."

"What happened?" Ebony asked, taking the tray of food to the table.

"Had somebody been answering their phone, they'd know," Quita chastised.

"I'm sorry," Ebony said.

BJ prayed Ebony didn't have a fit that she wasn't involved, but to BJ's surprise, Ebony's eyes clouded with tears. "I'm so sorry I wasn't there for you. Oh, God. You must have been going crazy. Everything okay now?"

Quita and BJ looked at each other.

"What the hell is wrong with you?" Quita demanded.

Ebony looked truly alarmed. "N-nothing."

"You're being too nice. What's wrong? Your mother dead or something?"

BJ banged Quita on the arm. "That was not funny."

"Sorry." Quita's cheeks flamed red and her eyes were just as blood shot. The last few days had taken their toll on all of them.

"I met someone," she said. Ebony leaned in to talk confidentially when her cell phone went off.

Everyone in the dining room looked up. Unaware of the no-cell-phone policy, Ebony answered. "Stan? What's wrong? I'm on my way." She grabbed her purse and half-eaten banana. "I've got to run. Stan's crashed the computer system or something."

They both watched their friend, who'd transformed into a self-assured and much less hostile woman.

"Who are you?" Quita wanted to know.

Ebony burst into a big smile. "It's me all right, but we'll have to talk details Sunday. By the way, our stocks split on ESX. Call me if anything changes with Granny."

"Hey! You were with a Realtor today," Quita exclaimed. "You're full of secrets."

Ebony hustled away. "Sunday," she promised.

"That's good news about the stocks. I haven't been paying much attention lately. You?"

"No," BJ admitted. Her mind couldn't handle another thing.

She and Quita sagged against their chairs. "I'm glad at least one of us is getting some action."

"Speak for yourself," BJ told her.

"You, too? The cop?"

"We did, but he's a jerk," she added softly.

"Stop," Quita sympathized. "Wouldn't that just be the case? The one guy you let in is a clown. But I suspected that he would be."

"Based upon how we met?"

She nodded. "I broke it off with Jimmy."

BJ sighed. "He was around a lot longer than I expected."

"He was getting too needy. Too available. He called today to ask me how was my day." She shivered. "Yuck."

BJ poked her in the side. "You know there's something wrong with you when you dump a man for being thoughtful."

"It's not that. We both like sex, but that's the extent of our compatibility. He doesn't watch baseball, or basketball."

"You hardly watch either."

"I can hold an intelligent conversation about basketball with you, and you're an expert."

"Well," BJ had to agree. "So, how did the staff respond to your call?"

"Most everyone was okay, but Etta and Carmella were the angriest. They got a two-dollar raise."

"Damn. I should have stuck Robin up for a raise after I got mugged."

Quita's smile held no humor. "I don't know how that's going to work out. Those newspaper interviews didn't help. Vultures."

"The good thing is that you're now yesterday's news."

"That's a relief."

"Everybody else is cool?"

Her eyes shrouded. "All except one. That damn driver. He pissed me off so bad, but he gave me the time frame to look at on the tape. I saw *him* on the tape. He'd been having dinner at the restaurant. I guess I owe him."

"You guess? Girl, you need to learn how to eat crow. Why don't you just apologize, say thank you, and go on your way?"

Quita really looked perplexed. "That wouldn't suffice for him."

"If things are still frosty in a couple weeks, throw a party at your place and invite everyone, including him. Show them how much you appreciate them."

Quita's gaze was off in the distance, still focused on the man who'd stood up to her. "A party is a good idea. If we make any money this week, maybe I'll throw one. You're good to have around. Oh, my doctor's appointment is today."

"Quita—"

"I know. You stay here with Granny. Why do you think they're keeping her?"

"I don't know." BJ had been wondering that herself. All she could surmise was that they were being extra careful. "I'm going to find her doctor as soon as we leave and have a conference with him." BJ saved the uneaten food. "I might want this later."

Quietly they walked back to the elevators. "I think I might stop by to see my cousin Ivy, since I've got some time to kill. Call as soon as you know something," Quita said.

"You, too." Upstairs, BJ slipped inside and made her way to the easy chair when the older woman stirred and blinked awake.

"Joan, didn't I ask you to bring the clothes in off the line? They don't stay clean if the smog from the cars gets to 'em."

Shocked, BJ sat. Her grandmother had never mistaken her for

her mother before. Was she just talking in her sleep? Why was she thinking about her long-lost daughter? BJ had told the girls she hadn't known what happened to her mother, but she'd lied. Joan Jason had called one day when her baby girl was five years old and said she wasn't ever coming back. Raising a kid wasn't what she'd wanted to do with her life. Granny and BJ had been together ever since. So why was Granny thinking about her now?

"Granny, it's me, BJ."

Brown eyes opened and smiled at her. "Joan, she's all growed up. She'll forgive you. I know she will." Granny's eyes closed.

BJ looked at her grandmother's serene face and wanted to scream.

Had her mother returned after twenty-five years? Or had her grandmother become Alzheimer's next victim?

She hurried out of the room in search of the doctor. She needed answers and she needed them now.

Chapter 23
Quita

Doctor Amir Buzu walked into his office with Quita's file in his hand.

"Am I a good candidate for in vitro fertilization?"

"Yes. You've met all the criteria."

Her inner rejoice was short-lived. "Not in finances."

The doctor never even flinched. "That is up to you. You have a certain lifestyle. What are you willing to sacrifice to have a baby?"

She sat there, speechless.

"Ms. Snell, having a baby requires sacrifice. Now is where it has to begin, or you shouldn't have one."

She knew all that. "When can you begin the procedures?"

"You're in excellent shape. You can begin the shots right away. We've been through all the other procedures. You signed everything, I believe." He leafed through her file. "Yes, it's all here."

Her heart hammered. She was finally on her way. She wanted to be outwardly joyous, but couldn't.

Dr. Buzu looked at her and she was scared. "I'll see you in four weeks."

"Thank you."

Quita walked out, her head full. Before her doctors appointment, she'd visited Ivy and her rambunctious children and all she could do now was yearn even more. Visiting hadn't dissuaded her in the least.

Yet she knew she wasn't ready. There were so many decisions to make, so many things she had to do. She said she wanted a baby, but she had nothing—no clothes, no nursery, nothing but the desire in her heart.

From a side door, she watched Dr. Buzu exit and get into an old model minivan. She'd seen the picture of his four toothy children. *Braces*, she thought and finally let a dribble of joy invade her heart. She'd do the right thing. But sacrifice?

The doctor pulled out and she looked at his old van and she wasn't thrilled. There probably wasn't even a CD player in there. Could she trade her Benz for a minivan? Or Hennessey and apple juice for chamomile tea?

She was starting from scratch. But she didn't panic.

She had so many books and baby catalogues hidden in the bottom drawer of her bureau, as soon as it happened, she would start decorating.

Now she needed a good budget. Quita squinted into the sun. She'd never budgeted before. Would she be poor? No, but the money from the investment club would have to come out.

A thick pounding filled the right side of her head and wouldn't stop. What the hell was this? She looked at the line of traffic on I-20 and was glad she didn't have to drive to work on the highway every day. She'd be permanently enrolled in road rage classes.

Twenty grueling minutes later, she pulled into Upscale and counted the cars in the parking lot. Fifteen in all. They were usually packed by six-thirty on a Friday evening. Dismayed, she strolled through the parking lot instead of entering through the back. The customers needed to see her.

Etta rushed up to her. "This is disastrous. They're complaining about everything."

Quita quieted her with a hand on her arm. "Never on the floor, understood?"

The young woman nodded, mute.

"Relax, smile. Walk with me."

As Quita walked to each table, she chatted with the customers, making their children laugh and the guests at other tables eager for her to lavish attention on them.

Two tables away, grandparents were visiting and she sent Etta for the camera. "We've got to make memories."

Instead of flirting with the grandfathers, she teased the grandmothers about raising such good families and pretended to sit on their laps so they could adopt her. They loved her.

After the desserts and complimentary Polaroid pictures, the families paid their bills and left the servers hefty tips.

When Quita and Etta were done, the younger woman had worship in her eyes.

"I can't believe how you turned the whole night around. You were amazing."

"You want to know a secret?" Quita offered.

"Yes," Etta said eagerly.

"Make friends." Quita beckoned Rocky, who came toward her. "Treat them better than family. If you genuinely like people, they'll know and they'll respond."

Etta nodded. "I'll do better."

"Etta?" Quita said, and touched her arm. "You're doing great. Keep up the good work."

The girl beamed as she walked away.

Quita and Rocky were in the hallway before he spoke. "We're down two thousand and counting."

"I know."

"What's the plan?" he asked.

Quita wanted to tell him she didn't know, but her job was to be the idea person, and he'd helped bankroll the operation.

"I'm working on a few things, but my head is throbbing right here." She cupped the right side again.

"You never had a migraine before?"

Quita frowned. "No. Do you just start getting these?"

Rocky laughed and pulled her hand down. "When was the last time you ate real food minus the stress?"

"I can't remember. I don't think I've had vegetables in almost a week."

He ushered her inside her office and made her lie on the red leather sofa. He even tucked a small pillow under her head.

"Take a break. The floor is fine. The kitchen staff is good. Bingo's got the bar. I'll bring you some food. You need to eat." He entered her private bath and came out with a cup of water. "Take these."

Quita examined the red-and-white acetaminophen gelcaps and swallowed two of the three he offered. "I don't need that many. I'll be loopy."

"Take them anyway. To beat a migraine, you need something extra strong."

She sighed, too tired to argue. "Fine, but I have to get back onto the floor."

She lay back and closed her eyes while he rummaged in the closet. It felt good to just rest and have a man who had no secret motive take care of her.

Gently, he draped a chenille throw over her. "Bingo is lucky to have you," she said.

"I'll be back soon," he said so tenderly, she'd have thought he was talking to a baby.

Even as she rested, her thoughts were never far from the restaurant and her personal real-life drama. Now money and fear of failure, and too much thinking about a baby, made her head feel like it was going to explode. *Let it go*, a part of her said, and she did slowly. She dozed until her rumbling stomach interrupted her slumber.

Something smelled good.

Quita stirred and opened her eyes.

Mark, the Regal Liquor Distribution driver, was sitting in her guest chair, reading the newspaper. "How long have you been here?" she asked him.

"An hour."

She read her watch. Two hours had passed since she'd lain down. "I can't believe I've been asleep that long." She got up and the room started to spin. "Whoa."

He reached out and helped her. "Hey, sit down before you break something."

Little shock waves of awareness pulsed through her arm and back where he'd touched her. Their gazes met and held before she sat and covered her legs with the blanket. She reached for the phone on the end table.

"Do you need something?" he asked. His concern came as a surprise.

"Are you offering to wait on me?"

"Fuck no. You got enough of that going on."

Just that quickly, her ego deflated and her feelings were very close to being hurt. "What are you doing here?"

"I thought we could come to a meeting of the minds."

She folded her arms. "About?"

"I don't want to fight with you."

"You have a funny way of showing it."

"You still don't get it, do you?"

Quita held up her hands, then saw the serving tray and telltale silver plate cover. "I get it. Fine, truce. I'm starving."

She then remembered her pledge to be a nicer person. "Can I offer you something to eat?"

He folded down one section of the paper and picked up another. "Thanks, no. I just ate."

Quita lifted the stainless steel lid off and saw the ravages of her meal. "*My* dinner!"

He smiled and her stomach flip-flopped like a beached fish. "You were asleep." His grin appealed to the reasonable person she was when she wasn't hungry. Despite herself, she liked the red tinge of embarrassment that colored his cheeks. "I didn't want good food to go to waste."

"It wouldn't have if I'd been awake."

He shrugged. "You know what they say, when you're slow, you blow."

Less than amused, Quita considered him. "Well, I'm still hungry."

The paper came down. "Can you ask nicely?"

"Fuck no," she said, borrowing his phrase. "You ate my dinner. I'm not asking nicely that you replace it."

He sat there, and Quita couldn't believe he was actually thinking about whether he was going to get her some more food. She had to admit that although he was annoying, she liked that he didn't just jump.

Mark reached for the phone and asked Rocky to bring her another plate.

"You're not a delivery man," she said.

"How could you tell?" He sat with his legs propped wide, his fingers laced over flat abs. She inhaled his scent and her mouth watered. Quita didn't have instant-attraction episodes. This one had her perplexed.

"You aren't afraid of getting fired. Which means you—" dawning hit her. "You own some?" she asked, waiting for him to back up her assessment. "All?" she amended, to which he nodded, "Of the distribution for Regal."

"You're quick when you're hungry."

She rolled her eyes and kicked out her foot, which was shoeless. *Rocky.* She liked that his slow gaze started at the tips of her toes and ended at her eyes.

"I'm sorry," he said. "We called a truce. "Yes. I own the distribution arm of Regal Liquor Distribution."

"Why were you perpetrating like you were a real driver? Why were you checking us out?"

"Regal could be held liable for liquor usage if we know a shop isn't following the law. Consumers go after us after they go after the restaurants and bars."

"That's bull. You saw the inspector. They were ready to crucify us."

"You were in the right. It wasn't a witch hunt."

"You still didn't answer my question."

His gaze locked with hers. "I had my reasons."

"Did you get what you came for?"

Did he feel the static electricity between them? Or was she just searching for her next bedmate? A revolt waged inside, until she rejected that last thought.

"You throwing me out?"

"Why not? You could still have some ulterior motive, and since you're not telling me why you're here, so late, in my office, watching me sleep—" Quita knew.

Rocky knocked once and opened the door. "How's your head?"

"Fuzzy." She pointed to Mark. "You know who he is?"

"He told me last week while we were dealing with all the other crap. I knew something was up. He was too damn nosey."

Mark smiled at Quita and she ignored him. "You should have told me."

Rocky put down the tray and picked up the empties. "It was too late by then. Besides, you had other stuff on your mind."

Was he talking about the in vitro? She hadn't told anyone at work. She didn't want anyone to know until it was done.

"BJ's Granny got sick," Rocky said. "And all the other stuff . . . Eat before your food gets ruined," he ordered. "Then you're done for the night."

Quita breathed a little easier knowing her secret was still safe. "How are you trying to throw me out of my own place? Have all the men in my life gone crazy?"

"Just worried about you," he said, "besides, once you eat, you're going to be sleepy. Watch and see." With that, he left.

"He's right," Mark said. "The prime rib is good."

She didn't want to eat, out of defiance. "What are you looking at, Mr. Lying CEO?"

"Is that my new nickname?"

"If the uniform fits."

He grinned, taking the fun out of insulting him.

"You'd deny yourself food out of spite to me?" he asked, his voice filled with sexual awe.

Mischief and confidence lurked in his green-brown eyes. Quita got a sense that his power and confidence were intertwined in every aspect of his life. As it was for her. Except in one area. With men. She hadn't met her parallel yet.

"Still don't know why I'm here?"

The frequency of his visits, the way his eyes would stay on her until he left. She was achingly aware of why he was there. "No," she said, wondering why she wouldn't let the stupid game go.

He sat real close to her on the sofa. He was calling her bluff. Had she just played herself? A tickle ran up her neck.

She refused to draw her hands up or even acknowledge that he'd affected her by sitting damn-near on her lap. This game of chicken put her pride on the line, and she wasn't about to lose it.

She met his gaze confidently.

Mark inched closer until his chest was on her arm.

He smelled so damned good.

She didn't blink as he put his arm along the back of the couch. "Big decision." He studied her lips from inches away. "Food or Mark? What will she choose? Door number one or two?"

This is a game. But his eyes didn't hold a hint of amusement. He'd back down before she would.

Quita moved to within an inch of his mouth. Her eyes strayed to her plate, then back to him. "Guess it isn't you after all."

Before she could touch the stainless steel cover, Mark's hand was there first. All she could do was caress his skin.

The pounding in her head was joined by her galloping heart.

She drew her hand back and his trailed hers.

Flustered, she almost touched her thighs and didn't, her chest and didn't, her neck and didn't, her cheek—

He caught her jaw between strong fingers and made her look at him. "Are you still playing?"

She couldn't speak.

All she wanted was for him to kiss her and end the nonsense. She'd apologize and mean it, and go on with her life. She focused on the contour of his lips and the pink tip of tongue that peeked from behind pretty white teeth. "No."

He was a breath away, and her eyes slid closed.

"I'm not either." He got up and left.

Chapter 24

Quita

Quita liked being in Upscale when no one else was there. She walked around the restaurant, taking pleasure in the clean, quiet space. Last night when she left she'd been so overstimulated, that when she'd gotten home, only a cool shower could quiet her yearning. Mark. She sighed. The cause of one sleepless night.

Quita made herself walk around. He held the distinction of being the first man she'd wanted to make love to and hadn't.

She wasn't sure if that was why she wanted to see him so much, or if she wanted to be the one to walk away.

Her thoughts gravitated back to this Sunday's investment club meeting. It was important. They'd made a tremendous amount of money over the past two months. If they continued to choose well, they could liquidate some of the moderate achievers and still be on track to make money.

In her portfolio alone, there was enough for at least three in vitro attempts. If the restaurant rebounded as she hoped it would, she'd be set for the remainder of the year and would actually have savings.

The dating game was taking its toll on BJ, but Quita hadn't had a chance to feel out Ebony. She'd been AWOL this past week.

BJ had already spent two nights up at the hospital and Quita knew she was ready for some real food. She cooked for them and set the table with the newspaper and their portfolios so when the girls arrived, they could get down to business.

Quita heard them come in. "Lock the door behind you," she called, bringing steak and eggs to the table.

"This looks delicious," Ebony said as she waltzed in, a short skirt wrapped around her thighs.

BJ walked in, slower.

"You all right?"

"Sleeping in that chair bed at the hospital, and no exercise," she clicked her teeth. "Not a good combination. Ms. Sunshine here can't stop smiling." BJ nodded toward Ebony. "What's his name and does he have a brother?"

Ebony sighed, and the girls laughed.

Quita raised her eyebrows at BJ, watching Ebony. "He must have the golden rod."

"Quita," Ebony admonished. "Your mouth."

"Let's eat first and then get down to business." BJ dished up their plates. "What's his name and all that good stuff?"

"His name is Abel and he's a dancer."

"Wow," Quita said, impressed. "Is he with a company out of Atlanta?"

Ebony looked shy. "Not that kind of dancing, although he has some professional training. He's an exotic dancer."

BJ choked and Quita blew food out of her mouth. "You've got to be kidding. Where'd you meet Mr. Hot Pants," Quita asked after drinking a full glass of water.

"He was dancing at a club, and I went, and he danced for me, and we've been together ever since."

"Damn, aren't you the secret keeper," Quita commented. "And he's the reason we've had a hard time getting in touch with you."

"It's just that it's been a while since I've been with someone and I didn't want to sacrifice that time, although I didn't see him this weekend. I'm not like you two," she defended herself. "Men don't want me like they want you. I have to take attention where I can."

"That's so not true, because it's about attitude. But," BJ said, "Let's hold off on date night and do the business first. I don't know about you guys, but my financial situation is in the doghouse. Granny is still in the hospital. She's got high blood pressure and diabetes. I may need to liquidate my shares in the club."

Ebony's mouth hung open. "I didn't know she was that bad."

"They've kept her and have run a whole host of tests and have come up with those two things. But she's been very confused lately. I'm just saying I may need the money. Besides, the game is running me into the ground."

"I need the money, too," Quita said. "I need to get out of the club." Quita set her juice on the table and looked at both the girls. "In vitro is going to cost me a fortune. I need the money so that I can have all of the treatments. Hopefully one of the first ones will be successful, but I may need several. Maybe more than that. They cost between five and ten thousand dollars. I don't have that except with the club."

Ebony set down her fork. "I don't want to get out of the club. I don't make the kind of money you guys make. I'm a glorified secretary, and the money we've made is about one half of my annual salary."

"But, Ebony, we're not guaranteed to make more money. We could lose it all tomorrow," BJ told her.

Ebony nodded, looking scared. "But we haven't. Our investments are solid. We're doing everything right."

"So you don't care that we need the money?" Quita asked.

"I care, but we had an agreement, Quita. This is my money, too. I don't have to agree with your decision to liquidate. Can we please drop this and pick our new stocks?"

"We want out and that's our money." Quita threw her napkin on the table and glared at Ebony.

Ebony stood. "Our agreement says we can liquidate early, but only if you forfeit your investment. If either of you want that, then I win all the way around." She dropped her investment money of one hundred dollars in twenties on the table and started out. "Let me know your decision."

Chapter 25
Ebony

Ebony signed on to the system and prayed she didn't get kicked off again. A virus had shut down their computers on Friday, but she'd fixed them and returned to work as usual.

But a new virus released over the weekend had been eating computer hard drives, erasing data. She tapped the keys on her old laptop, a dinosaur compared to the sleek models available now. Although slow, within minutes she was online and at the website to download the patch. However, her old system didn't have the capability to handle getting the entire company computer system back up and running. They needed an IT person who knew networking for small businesses.

She flipped through her Rolodex, another dinosaur she took heat over, and found the computer repair company's number. She explained their problem and didn't like the news. "Stan," she called from her desk.

He came to the door, a worried look on his face. "What's up?"

"It'll be two days before they can get here. Apparently, this affected all Internet users with Windows XP."

He swore uncharacteristically. "That's not good enough. Forty percent of our orders come through our website. What are we supposed to do, shut down?"

Ebony sifted through her paper folder of warranties. "I knew I had it here. Randall," she said into the phone. "We have a service contract agreement with you for same-day service if the call comes before five o'clock. It's not quite five now—"

As she listened to Randall, Stan grew more agitated. Ebony hoisted her heavy laptop onto the desk. She needed to walk while she talked. "What do you mean our contract wasn't renewed?"

"Let him come when he can," Stan said and walked off.

Ebony felt herself getting angry. Why was he giving up so easily? "No, Randall. I wrote the check. Let me pull your folder. Hold, please."

She pulled the file and turned to a red-faced Stan. "You didn't maintain the coverage?"

"It seemed like a waste of money, considering we never used it."

Ebony's hand was up so quick, she rubbed her face and neck to disguise her urge to hit him. At the moment he reminded her of her mother. Backward thinking and cheap. Maybe she needed to be away from him, too. "Do you know how much this is going to cost, Stan? A fortune."

"I know," he murmured. "We never used it."

"That's the whole point of having insurance!" Disgusted, she stabbed the bleeping call button. "Randall, can you get here tomorrow? Not until after five? Fine. It's time and a half?" She glared at Stan until he grudgingly nodded. "Fine, someone will be here to let you in."

She ignored Stan as he stood between her office and his. This one incident wouldn't bankrupt them, but what else had he been skimping on?

"Ebony, I'll straighten this out with Randall tomorrow. And I'll restore our coverage, okay?"

Now he was acting like a child, like getting her permission after the fact would erase his cheapness.

Ebony didn't give him the satisfaction of a response. If he hadn't been paying off women, maybe his financial business wouldn't be so precarious.

She shut the laptop.

"Where are you going?"

"Never mind where's she's going," Penney, Stan's wife said from the door. She stomped in, hands on hips. Decked out in Dolce & Gabbana, Penney didn't look like she had a husband who was struggling financially. In fact, she looked just the opposite. And she was pissed. "Who is she?"

"Who?" he said, playing dumb.

"Don't insult my intelligence by lying. You tell me who Leah Waverly is or I start digging, and if I find—"

"Baby." Stan turned on the charm. "You can trust me. You're my one and only true love."

"I'm trip four up the aisle for you, darling, so I'm a little jaded, and I also know the signs of a cheating man. After all, that's how I got you."

Daamn.

Ebony watched the play-by-play and her thoughts tripped back to the letter and the check Stan had had her mail. He had a baby, but would Penney find out?

Ebony got her computer bag together. The couple would need room to fight or to make up. Either way, she didn't want to see it.

"Where are you going?" Stan asked Ebony.

"To a cube so I can try to recover the data on our computer."

Stan looked relieved. "You're the best."

Penney watched Ebony closely. She didn't have to worry. She had Abel and that's all the man she needed.

She was almost out of the office when she turned around, remembering something Quita had told her. "Stan, I have to have a raise."

Stan and Penney were well on their way to making up when he looked up in surprise.

"Reviews aren't until the end of the year."

"Over the years I've handled incoming orders, invoices, programming, I handle all the correspondence, making copies and keeping accurate records so none of us forget what we're supposed to be doing when. I'm not just your assistant, but I assist all the managers in this company. I even fetch coffee.

"I've been here fourteen years, Stan, since your dad was here. Now I'm your systems analyst, because you let the coverage lapse. I do a lot of extra work for you and Braeden, but I need a raise so my boyfriend and I can buy a house."

"Ebony!" Penney exclaimed, forgetting Stan for the moment. "I didn't know you were seeing someone."

"Me neither," Stan added grumpily.

"His name is Abel and we're trying to qualify for a house, so I have to add my fair share. I haven't had a raise in two years, and I think it's time."

"Two years?" Penney exclaimed again. Ebony wished she'd bring it down a couple degrees. "Stan, you're always complaining about salary demands. Ebony, I used to be a secretary. My boss was such a pig. I would juggle his women, reserve hotels, and sign the checks he'd send to pay off their abortions."

"Really," Ebony said, staring at Stan. "How miserable you must have been."

Penney leaned into Stan's inflated chest. He must have been holding his breath. "You tell me the minute you suspect he's messing around."

"Penney," he said, his eyes begging Ebony. "You're all the woman I need."

"I'd better be, love."

"Stan," Ebony said, while his nuts were still in his wife's vice grip. "My raise? I think forty-five thousand a year is fair."

"You're not making forty-five now?" Penney guffawed. "No wonder you dress—well, I know you do your best."

"I try, Penney."

Stan's face was so red, if a pore opened, he'd bleed to death. "We'll talk about it Monday."

"Oh, darling, give it to her. She's been here her entire adult life."

Stan said nothing.

"Honey?" Penney was waiting for an answer while Ebony's heart thundered. She knew his secrets and his look let her know he wondered what else she knew.

"Fine. You got your raise."

"Wonderful! Call me, Ebony. We'll have to have you two over for dinner."

"Dinner sounds nice, thank you. Maybe a day next month. I'll check with him and see what his schedule looks like."

Ebony was thrilled that she gave Stan a double shock with her new attitude and her new man. With her raise, she wouldn't have to tap her investment club money, which was multiplying like crazy. Her dull and dreary life had finally turned excitement corner, and she was hot on the trail of having what she always wanted.

And in time, Stan would come to accept her unexpected raise and the thousands of dollars this computer system was going to cost him, because he'd been getting off cheap forever. This time he'd rolled the dice and lost. She was glad to finally come up the winner.

Ebony settled in to a rarely used cube and double-checked her old system where she kept her backup files. She'd just backed it up the previous Friday, but Stan didn't know. She always kept one copy at the office and another one at home, just in case. She considered that *her* insurance policy.

Ebony got down to work and was able to restore two hard drives before she got cold. She reached for her coffee, and realized she wasn't at her desk. She stood and stretched. It was pitch-black outside. Everybody was gone for the day. She hadn't heard from Abel all day, even after he promised to call.

She dialed his cell phone but got no answer. No matter.

Hopefully he'd found a gig and had picked up a few extra bucks. She played the voice mail she'd saved. *"Baby, gone to Chattanooga to work for the weekend. Can't wait to see you Monday night."*

She packed up and as she set the alarm, wondered how Stan would get out of his fix with Penney. Obviously he was spreading himself too thin. Good, maybe getting busted by his current wife would teach them both a lesson about fidelity.

She hurried to her car, and shifted into drive when the left wheel dragged and the car wouldn't accelerate.

Ebony got out. In the dimness of the lot she saw the flat. "What the hell am I supposed to do now?" She went back inside and dialed Abel again. Then BJ and Quita. Nobody was around, and for a moment loneliness drifted in. "Please," she muttered, realizing she'd need something . . . anything.

It was after nine at night. There wasn't even a service station open at this hour. She'd have to call a cab. While she'd kept her Rolodex full of numbers, she'd never needed a cab before and had thrown out all of the phone books during the extermination a few months ago.

She dialed directory assistance and was connected. "What city?"

"Anyone in here?" a male voice called from the outer office.

"Me!" she exclaimed and hung up. "Who's here?"

"It's me," he said, as she ran out of her office. "Boyle."

"Oh, hey. Hi," she said, trying to sound nice. She was really glad to see him, yet she still wasn't sure of how he felt about her.

"Oh. Hey. Hi." He walked past her to the entrance.

Ebony trotted after him. "I already apologized. I'm sorry. Okay? Really, Boyle, please!"

Her intensity stopped him and he turned back. "What?"

"I'm trying to apologize. I really am sorry about what happened. Can we . . . be friends? I mean, why not? You don't believe in forgiveness?"

He held his composure for a moment, then softened. "Yes. You're forgiven. Good night."

Ebony couldn't let him leave her. She followed him to the door. He unlocked it and stepped out.

"I need help."

"I don't know how to fix computers, so—"

"I have a flat tire."

"What makes you think I know how to change tires?"

"You're a man!"

He shook his head and then smiled. He really was handsome. "In your hometown, they must have given men Michelins instead of baby rattles."

Her face flamed. "Can you help me or drop me off somewhere?"

"I'll drop you off. And if you don't have anyone else, I'll come back tomorrow and change your tire in the daylight. Okay?"

She wanted to hug him, but didn't want to chance getting on his bad side again. "Let me get my purse." Less than a minute later, she was out of the building, too.

Boyle's car was a late-nineties Volvo station wagon. A true family car if she ever saw one. But it was clean and she was glad to be mobile again. He didn't talk and she didn't either, except to give him directions to Abel's place.

Suddenly she remembered the lingerie in the trunk of her car. She smacked her forehead.

"What's wrong?"

"I left something in my car."

He slowed. "You need it tonight?"

"No, thanks anyway. I don't want you to go out of your way. I appreciate you giving me a ride."

"If you really need it, we can turn around."

She reached out her hand, then drew it back. "No, really. It can wait."

She gave him the rest of the directions, and could sense his wariness at the neighborhood.

"Who did you say lives over here?"

She wanted to lie and say her boyfriend, like she'd pretended with Stan and Penney, but she didn't want Boyle to think her man couldn't afford something better. "My friend. He's moving soon."

"Oh. *That* kind of friend."

A smile curved her lips. "So?"

"I just got the impression you were single."

"Why's that?"

"Ebony, you're a little uptight. In case you haven't noticed."

"So I'm not supposed to be with someone? I'll have you know he likes me for who and what I am."

"The saying is true then."

She felt a trap coming, but kept walking. "What saying?"

"There's someone for everyone." Boyle started laughing. Ebony had to convince herself not to be offended. "You're about as hilarious as a splinter in the eye. Pull over here. He lives upstairs."

Boyle parked and shut off the car.

"What are you doing?"

"If you think I'm letting you walk in this neighborhood by yourself, even up the stairs, then you don't know me. Oh, that's right, you don't. Stay in the car until I come open your door."

She exhaled sharply but did as she was told. When her feet hit the curb she glared at him. "Happy?"

"You're welcome, Princess Difficult."

Ebony didn't know how to respond. She marched up the stairs to Abel's house door. She knocked. The TV blared, but she didn't hear anyone. She knocked harder.

"I don't think anyone's home," Boyle said, standing too close to her ear.

"They wouldn't leave the TV on. It's the most valuable—" she stopped short. She couldn't talk trash about her man in front of another man, even one she wasn't interested in.

Ebony turned the knob and entered.

"Hey," he warned, "you don't just walk into a man's house when he's not expecting you."

She marched in like the militia. "We were supposed to get together tonight, anyway. Abel, sweetie. It's me, Ebony. Baby?" She called. She got to his room and opened his door.

A scream tore out of her mouth, as a searing pain blistered her chest. The tangle of humping bodies grew wild as the mad detangle began.

Ebony kept screaming, as legs and arms and appendages came into view. The more she saw the more shrill she became, until Boyle shook her and she bit her tongue.

Words wouldn't come, just unintelligible grunts. Stars shot into her eyes and her legs turned to rubber.

Boyle caught her behind the knees and hoisted her over his shoulder.

The last image Ebony remembered was of Abel, package deep, in another man, while another man was deep in him.

Chapter 26
BJ

"Your grandmother has Alzheimer's. I'm sorry."
The doctor waited for her words to sink in, but BJ had already suspected as much. Knowing didn't stop the pain, or the sense of loss that claimed her. Her eyes smarted and she wished she had someone to hold hands with just for a moment. She wanted another shoulder for this awesome burden of pain.

Doctor Stone came around her desk and took BJ's hands.

"Are there any other family members I could call for you?"

BJ shook her head. "No, it's just us."

"What about your friends? I can have my secretary locate one of them."

"Okay. But I just need a minute to get used to this. I was hoping it was something else. Anything—"

The doctor nodded, understanding.

BJ tried to keep the tears in, but finally gave up and cried. One day, she'd be without her grandmother. She'd never really thought about that before. Her grandmother had always been there for her.

Doctor Stone left for a few minutes and BJ pulled herself together. When the doctor returned, BJ had found tissue and dried her eyes.

"Your friend Marquita Snell is on her way."

BJ swallowed. "What are our options? Granny seems to have most of her thinking ability. How fast does this progress?"

"It varies. Actually, she's done quite well. But there were signs."

Now that BJ had done a little homework and was more educated about the disease, she had to admit there were. But her grandmother was seventy-eight. She was bound to forget things.

Sometimes BJ forgot things. That didn't mean she had Alzheimer's.

"She needs to be in a facility where she can be cared for properly. The Dunwoody Assisted Living Center is for independent seniors. Mrs. Jason has requested to go to Ashford Plantation, a facility for seniors with mild to moderate Alzheimer's. Apparently, she has friends there."

BJ got up and walked around. So Granny knew. Had she been keeping it a secret? BJ had intended to ask Granny about Joan, but now maybe she wouldn't.

"I don't know if I want her to go somewhere else. Maybe she should come home with me."

Doctor Stone clearly didn't think so. "BJ, caring for a senior citizen is already a big job, but caring for a senior with Alzheimer's is impossible if you don't have the experience or the time. You work full-time. What will she do all day?"

"I don't know." Frustrated, BJ stalked around the office. "I'll have to hire a sitter or something. I can't just put her somewhere. She didn't do that to me. I can't—" She choked up. "I can't do that to her."

"I'm going to say this and then I'm going to refer you to the hospital social worker. Adults take in children because they need help. Children are helpless beings who, with time, are going to become independent and self-sufficient adults. Caring for adults with Alzheimer's is caring for an adult who will revert to a childlike mind, but in no other way resembles a child. They cease being the loving individual you used to know and may become hostile, forgetful, angry, hypersexual, liars, or many other things, and they will never get any better. They will never return to the person you remember. Not ever.

"The disease is progressive and at this time, there's not a whole lot we can do, except give medications to slow it down. Your grandmother is in her right mind enough to know she wants to live with her friends. Never once did she say she wanted to live with you. While she can still make decisions, why not let her?"

The doctor's words ate at BJ's hope. Her grandmother could become a virtual stranger, but not in BJ's heart. "When I was with her yesterday, she thought I was my mother. We haven't seen her in nearly thirty years. Is it possible that she came back or was this some type of memory lapse or a dream?"

"According to the visitors log, besides you, your grandmother hasn't had any visitors except the pastor of her church and the mother's ministry deaconess. Seeing your mother is a manifestation of the disease. Let's get Sonia Baldwin in here. She's the senior social worker assigned to Granny's case."

BJ stood. "No. Not now. I need to think. Is there any reason we have to rush this discussion? Can we do this in the morning?"

"It has to be tomorrow. But in the interim, Granny is ready to be released. We have to know what you're going to do."

"She can't go back to Dunwoody?"

Doctor Stone shook her head. "Now that the diagnosis has been made, no."

"Well, can't she stay here for one more night? I'd take her home, but she could hurt herself."

"We can order another set of X-rays to make sure the bone is setting properly. But she must be released within twenty-four hours."

BJ shook the doctor's hand and was in the hallway when Quita hurried toward her.

"You look terrible," Quita said, and hugged BJ hard.

BJ held on to her friend for a long time. "She has Alzheimer's."

"Shit," Quita swore. "I'm so sorry, sweetie."

"I know."

Quita steered her into an empty waiting room and pulled BJ into a chair next to her. "Bad?"

"Not as bad as it can get. Granny wants to live with her friends at this other place, but I want her home with me."

"Why, BJ? You can't help her. You need money to have her at home or in a home."

"I know, Quita, but she's all I've got."

"Maybe by blood, but you've always got me."

"I know," BJ said around a sob. "I didn't mean it that way."

"Don't explain yourself; you're confused and hurt. Let's go see Granny. See what she has to say for herself."

BJ visited with her grandmother and saw nothing of the woman the doctor said she'd become. Several of her friends from the center visited her and caught her up on the happenings. She laughed with them and introduced BJ again to people she'd met a hundred times. The reality of that first real clue hit her hard. Granny had had this disease for a long time. She'd always smiled a lot and called everyone "sweetie" or "chile," but not their names.

Finally she told the old folks to go home, because she needed her rest.

When they left she focused clear eyes on BJ and Quita. "You two are quiet as church mice. What you got churnin' in that head of yours?" she asked BJ.

"What I'm going to do with you."

"Nothing I don't want, I hope."

"How long have you known, Granny?"

"When you're old like me and you live around other old people, you know when your mind is starting to change. I guess I knew about a year ago when you and Ms. Lady here came to visit."

"You didn't remember my name, is that it, Granny?"

"That's right. Don't to this day."

BJ was shocked to hear the admission. She'd just thought her grandmother had given Quita a nickname.

Quita leaned over and touched her brown-spotted hand. "I'll be hey, or hey you, or Ms. Lady forever if you want me to."

Granny and Quita laughed softly. "Ms. Lady works fine for me."

Granny leaned back in her bed and eyed BJ. "I still know your name, Beverly."

"You thought I was Joan yesterday, Granny. Has she come to see you?"

The smile faded from Granny's face. "No, but maybe one day."

The social worker walked in and BJ was glad for the interruption. She talked to Granny at length about her options and gave BJ brochures that she shared with Quita. When she saw the prices, BJ balked. "Five thousand a month?"

"That's pretty high," Granny said. "Do we get Jell-O every day?"

BJ glared at her. "For these prices, you should get Jell-O at every meal."

"You do," the social worker assured them. "Look over the entire folder and then call me tomorrow at noon. We can have Granny transferred into that facility or another and on a great program to well-being in no time."

BJ shook her hand. "Thanks. I'll be in touch."

These prices were more than she'd paid for anything in her life. She didn't have this kind of money sitting around. That was sixty thousand dollars a year. She made almost three times that, but she lived well, and caring for Granny these past couple years kept things tight. Where would she get the additional money on a continual basis?

"Go home, Beverly. Let God work this out."

Again, BJ was at a loss for words. She wasn't sure how God was going to handle this. Especially since she'd been bothering Him about a man a lot lately. She got up and she and Quita kissed Granny good-bye.

In the hallway they walked slowly, each lost in thought.

"Did life just get crazy in the past few weeks or is it me?" BJ wondered.

Quita shook her head, stalking down the linoleum in four-inch heels. "Must be a full moon every day this month because life is nuts right now."

They got into the elevator and out into the parking garage. "I'll drop you at your car," BJ offered. "Where'd you park?"

Quita looked down. "I got a ride."

"Oh. Your car okay?"

"Yeah."

BJ sensed Quita was stalling. "From who, since you haven't said already."

"His name is Mark."

BJ waited until the silence grew heavier than the heat in the car. She started the engine and turned on the air.

"What's so special about this Mark that you aren't saying?"

"Nothing," she said, attempting to sound offhand. "He's bold and aggressive and up-front."

"Sounds like my match with Riggs. Honestly, he sounds just like you."

"Thanks."

"You didn't like being with him?"

"We haven't gone there yet."

"Oh." BJ was surprised. "You sound disappointed that you haven't."

"I'm fine, Beverly." Quita slumped back into her seat. "No, that's not true. He got under my skin. He was there the night Salvo and his brother tried to sabotage me, and he saw the whole thing. Later we had words, but he was the person who gave me the time frame to look at on the video. He came by the other night and almost kissed me. And then tonight, I fucking propositioned him and he said no."

BJ stopped at the light and looked at her friend. "I think you should marry him."

"Are you trying to be funny? Because you're not."

They were quiet for a while.

"BJ?"

"Hmm?"

"He brought me over here in his distribution delivery truck."

BJ laughed so hard, Quita wanted to pluck her in the forehead. "Quit lying."

Quita's hand flew up. "Honest to God. Then he lifted me down like I was a doll, hugged me so hard, and pushed me into the hospital."

A car horn blared behind them, and BJ took off.

"He sounds like someone you need. Do you want him?"

"I don't know."

BJ merged onto I-285 and settled in for a long wait. "Do you like him?"

Quita shrugged. "No. But I do."

BJ started to laugh. "Okay, then."

"What you gone do about Granny?"

"Pray I can come up with the money or an alternative that will make her happy."

"I can't stand Ebony right now."

BJ shrugged, neutral. "She's got a right to her opinion. I need the money, too, but what can I say? She's trying to keep us on task. Have you had your date this week?"

Quita nodded. "With Mark. You?"

"No, but I'll figure something out."

They pulled up in front of the restaurant. "Want to come in for a minute?"

BJ shook her head. "I'm too tired. I'm going to bed."

Quita hugged her and got out. "Call me tomorrow. I'll go with you to get Granny settled in."

"You don't have to. I'll call tomorrow afternoon after you wake up."

Quita patted the car and waved her away. "Bye."

Driving home, BJ worked figures through her head, and no matter how hard she tried, she didn't have the money. There were other centers that were less expensive that her grandmother could learn to love. BJ didn't know what to think. She pulled onto her street and into her garage.

Inside the house, she walked through the dark and stared out over the basketball court.

Riggs's hands on her arms. His mouth on her neck. His eyes as he made her climax. The doorbell rang.

BJ knew before she checked that it was him. She also knew that she'd invite him in if she made it to the door. She went into the laundry room, sat on top of the washer, and waited for the ringing to stop.

Chapter 27
Ebony

Ebony couldn't stop crying. Everytime she closed her eyes, she saw the man who couldn't make love to her, ass clenched, forward thrust—in another man. Her eyes hurt, and shame at her stupidity invaded every inch of her body. What had she been thinking that a man as handsome and virile as Abel could want her? He'd played her. His false sincerity rewound in her mind like a bad song, his earnest looks and gentle strokes all lies.

This past week she'd spent way too much money. She'd met their every need from food to household essentials. She hadn't been able to stand his bathroom and had cleaned it spotless, and had then bought new lingerie thinking he would get excited for her, when in fact that would never happen. She replayed in her mind the image of him hard and long. He'd known he was gay, so why mess with her? The truth slapped her. He wanted an ugly sugar mama.

She kept her hand to her mouth and stared through a sea of tears at the passing green streetlights.

"Where do you want to go?"

Ebony realized she was with Boyle Robinson, her savior three times over. First the letter, then the tire, and now this.

In the height of her snobbish stupidity, she'd dismissed and threatened the one man who'd been there for her every time she needed someone. What if he pulled over and told her to get out? Then she'd truly be alone.

"Maybe to your mother's house?" he offered.

A fresh sob shook her. "My mother hates me."

The thought of taking something so intensely personal, so painful, to Ruby Dee never worked its way into Ebony's realm of possibilities. "Can we just drive for a little while?"

"What about a sibling?"

"I don't have any."

"Best friends?"

"They're mad at me." She was imposing. He didn't want to be with her either. Sobs shook her chest.

The car slowed and she panicked. He was going to put her out. She'd finally estranged the last person on earth who had been kind to her.

"Ebony, I can't drive around burning up gas. I don't have it like that." Ebony gathered her purse in her lap and wiped her eyes on her suit sleeve. "Where are we?"

"Downtown Atlanta."

She acclimated herself and pointed. "Can you drop me off at the Residence Inn?"

"There's no one you can spend the night with?"

She shook her pounding head. "No."

"Your friends might be angry, but they're not so mad that they wouldn't take you in."

"Boyle, please. I don't feel like explaining everything to anyone. I'm already embarrassed and I'm tired." She took the box of tissue he offered and wiped her nose. "I just want to go to bed. Please."

He put the car in gear and drove in the opposite direction. "You can stay with me tonight and figure out what's what tomorrow."

She would have objected, but she didn't want to be alone.

Her eyes burned, but the stream of tears finally slowed to a trickle. She still wouldn't close her eyes for fear of the image burned there. "Thank you."

Boyle lived in Gwinnett County, off Jimmy Carter Boulevard. A security gate protected the property entrance and he stopped to use his key card to gain access. She wanted to ask why he lived way over here, but didn't. Her life had just been blown apart and the last thing she wanted was for him to think she was judging him.

Quietly they entered the apartment, and he turned on the lights. The living room/dining room combination was empty of furniture, but held a workhorse and several power tools, but no moving boxes. A small boom box sat in the corner plugged into the wall.

"I sold just about everything except my tools, but I just purchased the most important piece of furniture a man could own."

She didn't see a TV anywhere. "What's that?"

"A bed."

He dropped his keys onto the counter and pointed to their immediate left.

"Kitchen. The bath and bedroom are here."

He turned on the light to the bedroom and Ebony followed him in. A massive bed claimed the beige floor space while a huge headboard filled the wall.

Why had he invited her here if he only had one bed? She wasn't sleeping with him.

"If you have a blanket, I'll bunk in the living room," she offered.

Boyle didn't speak.

"I appreciate your hospitality. I promise I'll only stay for one night."

He finally looked at her. "You're not sleeping on the floor like some human reject." He went to the closet and opened the door.

Ebony checked her surprise. It was filled to the brim with stuff. Just like hers.

He pulled out what looked to be bound plastic. Picking up three bags, he grabbed her arm and walked back into the living room.

Once he pulled the cord on the first blue bag, it inflated into a twin size bed. The second bag inflated to a full size bed, and he told her to hold the flat side of the wide green nylon cloth. "Flick this up now!"

Ebony flicked and was startled to see the form shape into a tent. They laid it on the floor. Now Boyle had furniture.

Despite herself, she giggled.

Boyle's face settled into a soft smile. "I knew there was one in there somewhere." He smacked his hands together. "You can have the bed in the room—"

"Thank you, this is more than fine."

"I'm not done. There's a door, so you could have your privacy. But you wouldn't be having the fun you're guaranteed to have if you were out here in this roomy tent." He shoved the twin bed inside. "Notice how it zips. Privacy insured. But you could still talk to me because I'll be out here on this very spacious and firm bed. I've got a bad back. So it's me in the room on my expensive firm bed, or out here with you."

Ebony swallowed, choked up. "You don't have to watch me. I'm not suicidal."

"But you are sad, and you're beating yourself up for not knowing something you couldn't have known. So, you're stuck with me. Hey, you're in luck. I just bought some new boxer shorts."

Ebony couldn't follow his train of thought for being mentally exhausted. "What's that supposed to mean?"

"Once again your mind is in the gutter." He said the words as if there was no hope for her. "You can shower and wear them, and I'll get you a T-shirt. I'll put the clean clothes in the bathroom and then start some dinner. I don't know about you, but I'm starving. Come this way."

He left her outside the bathroom and entered and exited twice before gently pushing her inside. "Don't use all the hot water," he said, and closed the door.

An hour later, Ebony lay inside the tent on her borrowed inflatable bed, smelling of Johnson's Baby Lotion and Crest. Her stomach felt full, although she'd only had a couple bites of the Campbell's Chunky Classic Chicken Noodle Soup and red Kool-Aid.

She turned onto her side and listened to the ticking kitchen clock, and the tap-tap of the ceiling fan cord as it touched the globe after each spin.

The time for tears had long passed, but now the soul-searching had begun. She didn't like her mother and was fairly sure her mother didn't like her either.

She liked her job but not Stan's questionable business practices and his unstable bottom line.

She liked the idea of going back to college, but didn't have the time or resources.

She loved her friends, but was sure the divide she'd wedged between them was impassable.

She finally confronted the one question she had to give serious consideration to in the pitch-blackness. *Do I like me?* Her eyes smarted. *No.*

"Could you keep it down over there, I'm trying to sleep."

Boyle's voice startled her morose thoughts. "I'm not doing anything."

"You're thinking and your brain waves are interrupting the nonsensical but valid thinking I'm doing over here."

Ebony smiled and folded her hands on her stomach. "What are you thinking about? Paper or plastic?"

"Plastic. Makes good lunch and garbage bags. See the important work being done over here?"

"The fate of the world should rest in your hands," she told him.

Boyle's distractions helped her body rest and helped her come to acceptance of her current life situation one second at a time.

"Can I ask you something, Ebony? Or will you start crying?"

"I'm a river run dry." Ebony felt she owed him a few answers. "Ask away."

"Why did you call yourself stupid back at his house?"

189

"It's a long story, one I'm sure will bore you to sleep in five minutes."

"I don't think so, but try me. If you feel like it," he added.

"There once was a little brown girl who wasn't tall enough to be a model, exotic enough to be chosen for the elementary school picture board, smart enough to win scholarships, or attractive enough in high school to get boys she wanted to date. One day she looked up and she was twenty-nine. She hadn't had a date in fourteen months, so she entered into a pact with two friends to go on one date a week."

Ebony stopped talking and could hear his even breathing in the virtual silence. "Go ahead," he encouraged.

She debated continuing. Her life was a mess. Did she really want to expose all her sores to a man she worked with?

"I'm not judging you," he said in answer to her silent question.

"At the time it seemed like a good idea. And after a couple weeks, she went to a club where dancers perform."

"You'd never been to one before?"

"No," she whispered. "I wanted to be daring and do something on my own, but I guess he turned me out. We'd tried to—" she hesitated, not wanting to share the horror again. "But we never could."

"*He* never could."

"Now I know why."

"So back to my original question. Why call yourself stupid?"

"I should have known."

"What, that all male exotic dancers are gay?"

"They are?" Shock crept over her.

"My point exactly."

Ebony saw the finely woven box he'd gotten her to climb into and conceded. "I feel like all I've been doing is making bad decisions, and I don't know how to break the cycle."

"I've had some experience there." He sounded forlorn for a moment. Compared to her, he was a rock. "The key is to consider all the possibilities—pros and cons—without being emotional. Then think, what's the worst that can happen? Then, what's the best that can happen? Then make your decision."

"That sounds easy. Too easy."

"It's one of the hardest disciplines a person will ever have to learn. Go to sleep, Ebony."

She mulled over his words. He made more sense than anyone she'd listened to recently, including herself.

"Thank you, Boyle."

He didn't answer, so she assumed he was asleep. Soon, she drifted off, too.

Chapter 28
BJ

BJ sneaked into work early Wednesday morning and headed up to her office. It seemed like forever since she'd been behind her desk, and she missed it. Although she'd been away for just a few days, work hadn't slowed as new projects filled her in-box and an uninterrupted stream of e-mail from Robin filled the subject line. She caught up on the posts to distract her mind, but found herself drifting to thoughts of her grandmother's care.

Folders from four highly recommended centers for seniors with Alzheimer's were spread across her desk. They all offered various services, and ranged in price from moderate, like what she was paying now, to superexpensive.

The program her grandmother spoke the most highly of was the most expensive. BJ didn't see any way she could afford it and maintain the life she wanted for herself.

But of course that was an exaggeration. She didn't really need a four-bedroom home with a basketball court and custom-made closets. She could live without a two-car garage. She only had one vehicle and no lawn mower because she had a lawn service cut her grass. She could not shop for two years and still have enough clothes and shoes—and her sneaker fetish? She didn't need a new pair every month; she wasn't playing ball anymore.

Plenty of people lived in smaller homes, with basketball courts in their subdivisions or at the local health club, and they were perfectly happy.

But she wouldn't be. Not after working so hard to get where she was today. BJ knew that, but she didn't know how to break the news to Granny without breaking her heart. Granny had given her everything, struggled and sacrificed for her benefit, and now she needed BJ to sacrifice.

Did sacrifice have to require pain? Somehow BJ didn't think there was one without the other.

She leaned back in her chair, staring out the window.

"Glad you're alive."

Riggs.

BJ pushed on one toe and spun her chair around and faced him as he stood in the doorway. "Robin let you up?"

He nodded. "You've been avoiding me."

She nodded.

"Why?"

"Because I don't like you, Riggs."

"Ouch, that's honest. Can I ask why?"

"You used my unmarried status to try to debase my opinion of how you treated your ex-wife." BJ left it there. She didn't want to engage in a drawn-out discussion of how she wanted to be treated. He'd already made her feel weak and unimportant; she didn't need him to further demoralize her.

"I can be an asshole sometimes. I thought we had something."

"We do. *We did,*" she said, her gaze never leaving the handsome face she wished housed a different man. "You'd hurt me, Riggs. Over and over again, and I'm already dealing with too much pain. I don't need your crap." She blinked away his features. "I just don't need it."

"Your grandmother?" he asked softly.

"So you finally believe me?" He moved inside her office and sat down.

"I believed you that day." He grinned. "After you'd driven off and left your garage door up."

BJ shook her head. "I never even realized that." She knew he must have closed it. It was closed when she'd gotten home.

"I'm a fair listener," he offered.

BJ didn't want to be sucked in, but what was the harm? Riggs wasn't going to get to her anymore.

"She's got Alzheimer's. The facility she was living at can't take her back and the place she wants to go to is too expensive. Five grand a month."

He whistled. "What's your decision?"

BJ rubbed her temples. "I don't want to disappoint her."

"But you can't drop five grand a month on her."

Her chest ached. BJ felt as if she were disrespecting her grandmother. "Don't make it sound like that. I would, but I'd have to sell my house, car, everything. There are other places. They're just as nice." Her face crumpled and the tears fell into her hands. "I don't know what to do. I'm scared that she'll die and I'll regret not having made the ultimate sacrifice for her."

Riggs's hands massaged her shoulders. His voice was close to her ear. "The ultimate sacrifice is your life, and no one is asking you to give that up." He spun her chair around. "Look at me, BJ."

She finally did and read years of compassion in his eyes. *God, I could love him.* "A smart woman once told me she thought my ex-wife and I did what we thought was best for our daughter. Ultimately, we did and she's the better for it. I'm going to offer her that same advice to her for her grandmother."

"Why are you such a moron? We could have been good together."

He bent down and kissed her tenderly. "It's a flaw that's part of my DNA. You're a smart woman to know in advance what you can't deal with." He waited a beat for her to assent, but she could see herself giving in for the rest of her life. Relationships weren't supposed to be one-sided. "I still want to be your friend. Call if you need me." He squeezed her arms and then left.

BJ dried her tears and picked up the phone. Her grandmother was going to have to learn to love the center she'd chosen. And if she didn't, they'd cross that bridge when they got to it.

Chapter 29
Quita

The needle to the fleshy part of her right butt cheek hurt like hell. Quita held her breath as she administered the plunger and withdrew it. The nurses said she'd get used to it, but for a while it would be awkward and uncomfortable, especially since she was administering it herself. She disposed of the syringe and stowed the medicine and went back to the waiting file folder of information regarding donors. There were so many men to choose from, their profiles began to blend in her mind. She realized she was tired. She closed the files and took a seat on the couch to watch their stocks' gains and losses.

ESX pharmaceuticals had tanked, the CFO gone with the assets. In just a matter of days, they'd lost six thousand dollars. The thought of losing more brought pain to her frontal lobe, but Quita tried not to dwell on it. The stock market was a high-stakes lottery game, a risk she'd known going in.

What bothered her most was the notion that Ebony potentially stood between her and her dream coming true.

She'd had to triple her efforts at the restaurant and in the community. She was exhausted, anxious, and frustrated physically and sexually. Her self-imposed celibacy had been interesting in the beginning, but was now something that nagged her like an impossibly high itch on her back.

She twisted on the couch, careful not to press on her sore hip. *Mark.* She sighed.

He'd been sending his regular driver to make the deliveries. But that hadn't stopped her belly from clenching just a little every time she heard the hand truck outside her office door. She'd strain to hear his voice, then adopt an aloof demeanor all for nothing. He didn't even come to Upscale to eat anymore.

He knew he'd gotten under her skin.

She needed to talk to someone to get him off her mind. Quita picked up the phone and dialed BJ. "Hey, girl. Granny liking the new place yet?"

"No, but she'd better start liking it for twenty-five hundred dollars a month." BJ's frustration rang through her voice. She'd been at the new center for two days, not wanting to leave Granny. Personally, Quita thought Granny was acting spoiled, but those two had to work it out.

For the next six months BJ planned to take the money from her savings account and then start using her investment club money to pay for Granny's new accommodations.

Quita felt sorry for BJ. It was a lot of money, but no more than she'd been willing to spend to have a baby. "She's only been there two days." Quita tried to ease BJ's mind, something she'd been doing a lot lately. She felt like such a big sister. "Give it a chance."

"That's what I keep telling her."

"She'll come around." Quita shifted on the sofa. "Tell that old woman I'm coming to see her tomorrow and she'd better have a smile on her face."

BJ relayed the message and Quita heard nothing. "Tell her again, and then add 'damnit!' "

BJ repeated Quita's words and Granny cracked up. "Ms. Lady is so funny."

Quita giggled, too. "Well, I was just checking on you. See you tomorrow. Bye—hey!" Quita said.

"What?"

"Have you heard from Ebony?"

"Not since the meeting. I figured she's been with her man. Quita, I think she's right. I know you saw that ESX took a beating."

"That's one treatment for me, BJ."

"And two months here for Granny, but we can't look at it like that. My situation is my fault, really," BJ confessed. "We shouldn't have ransomed the club for date night. I'm not dating anyone and it feels damned good."

"Don't cuss in here," Granny said.

"Oh, Quita can cuss and not me?"

"Ms. Lady is one step from being the devil's mistress. We both know that. Oh, good. *Wheel of Fortune* is coming on."

Quita and BJ burst out laughing. "I think Granny is back," Quita said. She could hear BJ getting up as her eyes slid closed. Quita stifled a yawn. A nap would be wonderful.

"Granny," BJ said, getting up, "I'm coming right back."

"Fine with me. Tell Ms. Lady to bring me some candy. I can't stand the candy they got in here."

"They're giving her candy?" Quita asked.

"No, that's why she's complaining." BJ sighed in Quita's ear. "I haven't told Granny yet, but I've decided to sell the house."

"Like hell you are."

"Quita, I have to think past today and next month and even next year. It's just a house."

Sadness invaded Quita because she knew how much owning that house meant to BJ. She could see BJ sacrificing the car or clothes or something else, but the house represented her success and her passion. "You love that house, BJ."

"Well." She was quiet for a long time. "I can love living somewhere else."

"Are you sure?"

"Yeah."

"God, we're growing up. I don't know if I like it."

BJ chuckled. "I'm just glad I can take care of her. Know what I mean? I have some good news," BJ said, steering them away from the sad topic.

"What's that?"

"Ms. Mayline Venice's daughter found out Granny was here, and she started looking into transferring her mother here. Maybe they can hang out together."

"That's great. They can watch out for each other."

"Now that I think about it, I'm going to make a bunch of phone calls. If she can't live with them, they can come live here with her."

"You're a good granddaughter."

"I know."

"BJ, right?" a man said. "It's me, Tim."

Tim's rich voice conjured up images of Mark in Quita's mind. She eavesdropped shamelessly.

"Oh, hey." BJ sounded surprised and pleased. "From Hairiston's. How are you?"

"Good. I didn't mean to interrupt your call."

"Oh! Quita, I'll call you tomorrow."

"Call me tonight. Bye."

Quita set down the phone and closed her eyes, a smile on her face. Maybe two of the three would make a love connection after all.

She thought about calling Ebony, but let the nap she started have its way. Quita didn't drop off completely, but she would get some much needed rest. Sleeping at home without sex as a tension reliever left her tossing and turning in her bed.

Mark slid into her dreams. At the beach—she hated the beach. She saw him piloting a boat on the lake, swimming in the ocean, making love to her on the Isle of Capri. She sighed even in her dream.

"I can't barge into her office. She's asleep."

"She's just resting her eyes. She's going on the floor in fifteen minutes."

Quita stirred and recognized Bingo and Mark's voices. She pressed herself into the dream and wondered how Mark could be kissing her and talking, too.

"I don't know, man. Maybe she's not into white guys. Maybe she's got somebody already."

"Maybe you're a chicken."

"Bullshit." Mark was quiet. "I'm going in."

She sat up, unsure what to do.

"You're beautiful, you know that?"

Although she'd known he was coming in, the softness of his voice caught her off guard. She got up, and wanted to go to him, but she went into the bathroom and closed the door. When she came out dressed for work in a low-cut silk dress, he studied her. "Is that how you take all compliments?"

Quita had never been shy a day in her life, but she was tongue-tied and couldn't stand still. "No. Thank you."

She changed into different heels and applied gloss to her lips. She walked toward the door, expecting him to move.

"You're shy," he said, surprised.

She met his eyes for a second. "Not really."

"You are now."

She nodded slowly, staring at her shoes.

"Good shy?" he asked.

She nodded again.

"I'm a little shy, too." She looked up at him. "If you come a little closer, I'll reach for you."

Quita held back to catch her heart from falling first. "What do you want from me?"

"It's not obvious?"

"Sex?"

"Eventually."

That *was not* the standard answer. Her toe crept a little closer to the edge. "To ask me out?"

"You heard me out there?"

She nodded. "I thought I was dreaming. A date?"

He shook his head. "More."

Quita did something she'd never done before, she told on herself. "I've been thinking about you for days. I didn't think you liked me anymore."

He pulled her into his arms and she felt right at home. He moved with her, not dancing, but letting their bodies get in sync. "You're not a simple woman. I didn't want to blow it. Things had to be correct for what I wanted to do."

Their chests rose and fell together. "And what was that?"

She realized they were speeding through fifty dates, a hundred even, like they were making up for lost time. As long as he kept going, so would she. He had as much to lose as she did.

"Something big."

Her heart raced. Cautiously, she pressed her midsection into him and he pressed his lips into her neck. He was swollen between them. Impressively swollen. "Bigger than that?"

"Yes," he whispered.

"Oh God." She wanted to fly. Was he heading where she thought?

She nodded and a hiccup shook her chest.

"You're crying? Are those happy tears?" His breath hitched.

Quita let him go and was sorry to see hurt in his eyes. "Mark, do you want a family?"

"Yes."

She inhaled sharply.

"You don't?" he asked, looking at her. His fingers stroked her face.

"I do. Mark, I can't make babies by myself."

He didn't smile or crack jokes. He waited.

"I just started the in vitro process. I get the first insemination in three weeks."

He brought his arm up and cradled her head. He had amazing green eyes. These were the eyes of the man she loved. "It looks like I'm right on time," he said. "I've got all the sperm you need."

A relieved laugh burst from her chest.

Their mouths met fully in a loving kiss full of promises. She ran her hands through his soft wavy hair and couldn't stop herself from wanting to stay in his arms forever.

He laughed, too. "I wondered how many meals I'd have to have here before you noticed me."

"Poor baby." She loved the feel of his clean-shaven face against her hand. "Is this what you came here to do?"

He tipped her chin up and took a small bite. Quita purred. She'd never done that before.

"I want us to get married someday."

Her heart flew. "Yes."

They shared one of the longest kisses Quita could remember engaging in without following it up with sex. Somehow she knew they'd have no problem there. "We'll take our time," he promised.

"Yes," she said, her throat full of tears. He was what she'd been waiting for all her life.

"I'll love you forever."

Her hands roamed his body. "Yes, Mark. Yes."

"You don't know what the ring looks like," he told her, his voice sounding smoky. "The women in my family love big things."

"Even the ones that marry in?"

"*Especially* them. Quita." She loved the way her name sounded as it came from his lips. "I want you to be happy."

"I am. A big ring isn't what I want. A big heart? Well, that matters. Let me get Carmella and Etta to cover for me. You sit there."

He took the post on the sofa and she made her calls. While she had a minute, Quita called Ebony's home number. The girl was usually locked up in her bedroom at this time of night.

Mark's eyes caressed her as he watched her from across the small room. Quita could feel herself getting ready for him, but not here at work. She wanted to be able to enjoy him.

Ah, she thought, *another first*. His pleasure was important to her.

A prerecorded message played, saying that the phone had been disconnected. She tried Ebony's cell, which rang with no answer. "One more call, okay?"

"We have to leave now." He gently took the phone from her hand. "You can call from my house." His mouth caressed her. "I promise, but we have to leave before we don't make it out of here."

Her body tingled. In the past, Quita would have stood her ground, but she wanted to be with him. Now.

She got her purse. "I'm ready."

He opened the door and they left together.

Chapter 30
Ebony

Ebony awoke leisurely, cocooned in a warm blanket, birds singing outside the window. She stretched out, her arm seeking warmth from the body she'd become accustomed to, and met empty space.

Opening her eyes a crack, she saw the sea-foam green sky and was momentarily confused, until yesterday's horror came back.

Angling her body into a sitting position, she wished she'd slept through the difficult days ahead. But there was no escaping, not even in a waterproof nylon tent. The silver zipper beckoned and she didn't move to touch it. *Coward.*

But this wasn't the first time she'd chickened out on facing reality. She'd been actively dumb for weeks now.

There had been signs that Abel was just what he'd turned out to be, but she'd been too awestruck to admit it. She'd wanted to be like everyone else and stand up for her man with pride. Although his employment was smarmy and he was broke, she'd considered him a work in progress. She'd wanted to know what it was like to suffer through the tough times and overcome, and then tell her story of faithfulness and strength the next time a bunch of female ears were perked and ready to listen.

Just once, she wanted to hold her head up to Quita and BJ and show them that she was able to pull a man as handsome as Abel without her having been a mercy date for one of their male friends. She squeezed her body tight, fighting the last image she had of Abel.

Being with him had inflated her ego. She'd stood up to her mother, Stan, and her friends. But as her stomach tossed, Ebony knew what she'd done to BJ and Quita had been wrong. Greed and superiority were a toxic mix in the hands of someone who'd forever been jealous of them.

In the light of day, she knew Quita and BJ couldn't have changed the fate of their now prosperous lives any more than she could, but that hadn't stopped Ebony from using power to finally say the one word she'd been wanting to say to them forever: No.

She had to have a sickness, she thought now. There had to be something wrong with her. Quita and BJ had never done anything to her. Ever. But last Sunday she'd felt like God. She'd been so drunk on power, she'd left and spent a hundred dollars on silly things for her and Abel. Now she saw how much she'd lost instead of gained.

Ebony sighed and vowed not to cry. She created this situation. She had to get herself out of it somehow.

At least she'd gotten a long-overdue raise. She'd make sure her life changed for the better. *I'm a better person today than yesterday,* she said three times, cheerleading herself to unzip the tent.

Boyle wasn't in bed and she climbed out, the blanket robed around her from chest to ankle.

When she didn't find him in any of the rooms, she washed and dressed. Stowing the beds proved difficult, but she got them deflated and the tent flattened when she heard his key in the door. "You're up," he said, walking in.

"It's six forty-five. I usually leave home at this time."

He dropped white paper bags onto the counter and glanced around. "Breaking camp, huh? I'll put these away later," he said, referring to the beds. "Hungry?" He handed her a bag of food.

"Not really, but thanks."

"I always have a good breakfast," he explained as if it were an ordinary occurrence for her to be in his home. "Feed the mind so nothing gets past you. Let's roll. We can eat on the way."

Ebony followed, not looking at him. She felt funny leaving his apartment at this hour. The action implied intimacy, and there was none with Boyle. He didn't know a thing about her, yet he'd taken her in. She owed him a lot. His kindness said inexpressable things about him.

They got in the car and were under way in minutes. "Boyle—"

"The thing is, Ebony, from the day I met you, I felt a connection. Let's skip all the 'do you like sushi, and do I like steak,' 'I'm sorry for this or that,' and be friends just as we are, okay?"

Relief and gratitude flooded her. "Okay, friend," she said. "Can I add something?"

"As a friend, yes," he said, hitting his turn signal at Buford Highway.

"I don't like sushi. I prefer steak, and thank you for last night and for everything."

"Is that the last 'thank you'?"

She smiled and unwrapped a greasy egg sandwich with bacon on top. Her stomach rejoiced. "Yes."

"Good. You gone eat that?"

She bit into her meal. "You eat too much."

"Very good," he approved with a smile. "Friends talk about each other. You're catching on."

The computers were up and running like new when Ebony entered her office. The invoice rested in her in-box and she didn't break stride as she dropped it on Stan's desk. This was his company and his problem.

She sat down and called the Realtor, Gil Edison. "Can you search on property in the Fulton County area?"

"What price range?"

"One-fifty to two hundred?" she said hesitantly.

"If we can get you qualified for two-fifty, our options open up."

Ebony took a deep breath. "Let's go for it."

"Great," he said, a smile in his voice. No doubt for the healthy commission he stood to gain.

"When can we go out looking?"

"After five today, if you're available."

"I'm available after noon. Is that too soon?" she asked.

"Not at all. I'll e-mail you the listings and all the forms to fill out. Fax them back to me and we're on our way."

"Will do. See you at twelve."

She hung up and then pulled her checkbook out of her purse. She'd been meaning to balance it for days. She dialed the number and the code. *"This account is overdrawn fifteen dollars and twenty-four cents."*

Disbelief and anger hit her in the stomach.

Ebony pressed one and listened to the automated voice again. That couldn't be right. She had more than four thousand dollars in the bank.

Abel. Her purse missing from the bedroom. Him not wanting her to go get it.

She called the corporate office of the bank and asked for the manager. If he'd stolen her money, there would be hell to pay.

At the corporate office of the Atlanta People Bank and Trust, Ebony watched video of Abel and his friends making withdrawals from her account six times on six different occasions. They were shameless in their greed, running up the debt from the ATM machine to two thousand dollars. The other two thousand had come from fraudulent withdrawals from her card number at computer stores. She viewed the slips that were compiled in front of her.

"This is not my signature, and I didn't authorize these purchases. What is the bank going to do about this?"

The bank manager and the head of security stood near her, trying to look impartial. "Ms. Manchester, if you didn't give these men permission to use your card, how did they come to have it?"

The statement told the true story. Her purchase of one hundred dollars of fun at the Gigolo club was highlighted in blue.

"I do know him," she pointed to the frozen shot of Abel on video, "but I never gave him permission to use my card. We were together a lot. He must have seen me put in the number and he stole it."

A knock on the door caused everyone to turn. A black woman with straight black hair entered. "Another transaction is trying to go through now," she said to her bosses. "Shall I approve it? Fulton County PD is standing by outside."

"Where is he shopping right now?" Ebony asked.

"At Highland's furniture store. A twenty-five-hundred-dollar leather sofa, and—" she consulted the sheet in her hand—"a bed frame. You say you broke up with him yesterday?"

Ebony nodded.

"Guess he's going out with a bang."

Ebony turned to the two officers. "Will you believe me now that he's stealing from you?"

This galvanized them into action. Abel would be picked up as soon as he left the store and her money would be returned to her account.

Ebony stood and shook the woman's hand, and then her bosses'. She only wished she could have been there to see his arrest with her own eyes.

The black woman named Nisa walked her out. When they were out of earshot, she angled toward Ebony. "We met, but you probably don't remember me from Hairiston's. The dating night with your friend, BJ."

Her face did look familiar. Ebony shook her head. "I remember. I'm sorry we have to meet again under such embarrassing circumstances."

Nisa stopped at the outer door. "Please," she said, dismissing her apology. "How you spend your money is your business. Nobody has the right to steal it from you."

"What will happen to them?"

"They'll be prosecuted. No more dancing at Gigolo's for them. I also heard that Channel Two got a mysterious tip."

Ebony's mouth fell open.

"Close your mouth, I get around," Nisa told her with a smile that remained professional, in case anyone was looking. "That's the life of a single woman in Atlanta. Here's my card. I'll contact you tomorrow and you will have to complete a sworn affidavit."

"Thank you," Ebony whispered, close to tears.

"Don't cry," Nisa told her. "The bad guys are going down. The good guys won."

Ebony drove back to work and it wasn't until she parked that she realized her tire was fixed.

Boyle. She'd have to thank him. Somehow. Maybe someday there could be something between them. Ebony didn't want to rule it out. But she'd cross that bridge later.

Now she'd have to find somewhere to live and get her life back on track.

Ebony dialed Quita's number on her cell. She'd start by apologizing. If Quita told her to go to hell, well, she reasoned, she'd deserve it.

As the phone rang, Ebony prayed.

Chapter 31
BJ

BJ sat across the table from Tim Roth and sipped a cup of tea. She'd been so surprised to see him yesterday, she hadn't known what to say. But today they'd brought his mother and her grandmother together and the older women talked endlessly, which gave BJ time to focus on Tim.

"Are you sure your boyfriend isn't going to pop out of a closet and stroke your hair again?"

BJ laughed, embarrassed. "I'm positive. We're not dating. Anymore."

His eyes assessed her. "That's great news!"

The excitement in his voice made her laugh aloud. "You're funny."

"You still play ball?"

"Sometimes. Not as much as I'd like."

"Your grandmother is in a good place. My mother has been here for a year and she's doing well. You have to learn about the disease and make sure she's taking the drugs to slow the progression. Otherwise, she's just like everybody else here."

"I see that." They watched as his mother, Mary, tried to push

Granny in her wheelchair. They weren't getting far, but they had a good time laughing and talking as they went.

"They're adorable," BJ said, for the first time feeling at ease.

"You're not so bad yourself."

A real blush heated her cheeks. "You're just saying that."

"Fishing, are you?" He reached out and touched her hand. "How would you like to go one-on-one with the worst six-foot-five basketball player in all of Georgia?"

"Mmmm."

Tim started laughing. "You have a dirty mind. I like that!"

BJ laughed, too, her heart light. "I'd love to." Her cell phone beeped. "Excuse me for a second, please."

"What's up?" she said to Quita.

"Are you watching the news?"

"No, I'm talking to Tim."

"Tim from yesterday?"

"Yes, Quita. We're up here with his mom and Granny. What do you want?"

"Turn to Channel Two. I think Ebony's man is getting arrested."

BJ put her hand over the phone and asked Tim to turn the channel. They watched in silence as Abel Grooder was arrested for credit card fraud.

"Damn," BJ exhaled. "Have you talked to her?"

"No, she called yesterday, but I was busy."

"Doing what?"

Tim silenced the TV and watched BJ.

"I'm at Mark's house," Quita said.

"Work it sister," she said beneath her breath, giving Quita her blessings. "Look, I'll find Ebony. If I don't call within the hour, go by her place."

"Okay. If she needs me before then, call me back. Bye."

BJ hung up the phone.

"Do you have to leave?" Tim asked.

"I'm afraid so. My friend was dating that guy. I don't want you to think—"

Riggs's words about spending too much time with her friends ran through her mind. "She's a good friend. She doesn't have anyone else. I want to make sure she's okay."

"Do your thing. Maybe next week we'll have a chance to get in some basketball."

"Next week?" she said lightly, and scribbled out the directions on the back of her business card. "Tomorrow is good; that's if you're not busy. Besides," she added, flipping over his hand and laying the card inside, "I think you're lying about not being able to play."

"Does the loser get a consolation prize?"

BJ shook her head and stood. "No, the winner gets everything."

He got up, too. "In that case, I'll bone up on my game. Tomorrow."

BJ stepped around him, her body brushing his lightly.

Yes, yes, yes, she thought as she reveled in the electric heat that coursed through her. Tomorrow was looking like a wonderful day.

Chapter 32
Ebony

Outside of Ebony's house, a U-Haul truck sat at the curb. What the hell was going on?

Ruby Dee and Jo were standing on the lawn as two men hauled out the furniture, while two others carried boxes. Their movements were sloppy and hurried, and BJ knew something was wrong. She got out of her car and Ruby Dee hurried over. Her hurt knee didn't slow her down a bit.

"What you doin' here?"

"I came to see Ebony."

"She ain't here, so you can go."

The man coming down the stairs dropped a box and towels spilled out. Ruby Dee ran over, shrieking at him, glancing nervously at BJ. They were stealing Ebony's stuff.

BJ called 911 and kept her finger poised over the send button. "You've got to the count of three to unload anything that's Ebony's on that truck."

"She don't want it. She ain't been home in days."

"One, two, three—"

Ruby Dee screeched, but stopped the men from carrying out the rest of the boxes.

She hobbled to the truck and Jo climbed into her beat-up Sentra just as Ebony's car turned down the block.

Ebony jumped out and ran to BJ. She was out of breath, her hair flying.

"Ebony, it's just stuff. We can replace it."

"I don't care about that," Ebony said, with more calm than BJ thought any human capable of. Her mother didn't even give her a second glance.

"I'm sorry for what I did to you and Quita. If you never want to be my friend again, just know that I'm sorry."

"Eb. It's going to be all right," BJ soothed, as one of the neighborhood boys started picking up miscellaneous things Ruby Dee had discarded. He stacked the items on the porch and was soon joined by other kids who came to help.

Ebony watched as the young adults moved her towels and appliances from the porch to the kitchen counter.

"Thank you," she said and offered them money. They were hesitant, but she closed their hands around the bills. "Thank you."

After Ebony closed the door behind the kids, she and BJ moved into the kitchen. "My life seems like a train wreck."

"It's not. We still love you."

Quita burst in, Mark at her side, their hands clasped. "What the hell happened here? Cruella gone?"

Ebony nodded and started crying as Quita embraced her. "I'm sorry, Quita."

They held each other for a moment. "Me, too. Come on, let's sit down." They looked around at the trash-strewn floor. "Damn, she cleaned you out. Good. You can make a fresh start with new stuff."

"Hi, I'm BJ. This is Ebony." she shook Mark's hand and could see why Quita was so in love. Besides being handsome, he didn't disrupt and wasn't bothered by Quita's natural flow. He had his own. They were evenly matched.

Ebony shook his hand, too, but retreated fast.

"Bay," he said to Quita, who stepped to him in a second.

BJ perched atop the counter and adjusted to Quita being with a man in their presence. "I'm going to wait in the car. Ladies, it's nice to meet you."

Quita turned to them with a dreamy smile on her face. "Ain't he fine?"

BJ laughed and Ebony offered a small smile, but didn't comment. She was emotionally fragile, and BJ understood.

"We didn't come here to fawn over your man," BJ told her. "So get over yourself. Even though he's cute."

"Quita," Ebony said softly. "I was jealous of you. Of what I perceived you had. You, too, BJ. I got greedy, and"—she hiccupped and started to cry—"I'm sorry. We can dissolve the agreement and take our money. I'll understand if you don't want to give me what would have been my share. I'm sorry."

Quita's eyes were glassy, BJ thought, although through her tears she couldn't really tell.

"Whew," Quita said, sounding shaky. "I'm glad you got that out of your system. We're friends, Ebony. We're going to have rough times. I'm sorry I put us in a position where we had to choose."

"Do you really want out?" BJ asked Ebony.

Ebony gestured around. "I need the money to get my life back together."

"Well, I don't think we should dissolve," Quita said, much to BJ and Ebony's surprise. "I don't want to lose my two best friends. We're tight, damnit! And if we don't have the club, then what happens to us?"

"We're going to still be friends," BJ confirmed. "Nothing is going to stand in the way of that. But if you need the money, let's sell some of the stocks and use the money for what we need. But nothing is going to break us up. Not date night, investment club, stupid men, or men we may fall in love with. We're friends forever."

"I met a man," Ebony offered.

They both turned to her in surprise. "His name is Boyle and he's a good man, too. If I have any sense left after this life explosion, I'll do my best to hold on to him."

"You'll do fine," Quita assured her. "We're not going anywhere. BJ? What's up with Tim?"

"We have a date. Tomorrow. I'm going to beat him at basketball, and then I get the consolation prize. All six foot five of him."

They all laughed.

"I guess we're going to be fine," Ebony said, and walked them to the door.

"Are you showing us out for a reason?" Quita demanded as they stepped onto the porch.

"It's time for me to start getting my life together."

"I can stay and help," BJ offered.

Ebony shook her head. "I can handle this. I've looked forward to this day for a long time. I love you guys."

They hugged her, and BJ saw a man exit his car from across the street.

"Hi," he said as he passed them on the sidewalk. He bounded up the stairs to Ebony, put his arm around her shoulder, and they walked inside.

"Even without men, we'd be fine," BJ said to Quita.

"Yes, we would, but they sure make the ride interesting."

BJ couldn't help but agree.